Subroto Bagchi is chairman of MindTree, one of India's most admired software companies. He is India's bestselling author of business books, with titles like *The High Performance Entrepreneur, Go Kiss the World* and *The Professional* to his credit. His books have been translated into Hindi, Marathi, Malayalam, Tamil, Korean and Chinese.

MBA at 16 is his best-loved book yet, because he has always wanted to write a business book for young adults.

He lives in Bangalore with writer wife Susmita. They have two daughters, Neha and Niti.

MBA at 16

A Teenager's Guide to the World of Business

Subroto Bagchi

India's #1 bestselling author of business books

The High Performance Entrepreneur,
Go Kiss the World and *The Professional*

PENGUIN BOOKS

PENGUIN YOUNG ADULT

USA | Canada | UK | Ireland | Australia
New Zealand | India | South Africa | China

Penguin Young Adult Books is part of the Penguin Random House group of
companies whose addresses can be found at global.penguinrandomhouse.com

Published by Penguin Random House India Pvt. Ltd
7th Floor, Infinity Tower C, DLF Cyber City,
Gurgaon 122 002, Haryana, India

Penguin
Random House
India

First published by Penguin Books India 2012

Copyright © Subroto Bagchi 2012

All rights reserved

10 9 8 7 6 5 4 3 2

ISBN 9780143330974

Typeset in Sabon by Eleven Arts, Delhi

Printed at Repro Knowledgecast Limited, India

www.penguin.co.in

Contents

Acknowledgements

I am fascinated by the way an idea originates and, at times, develops a life of its own. This book is a case in point. One morning, on a visit to Delhi in the fall of 2008, I was having breakfast with my editor at Penguin, Sumitra Srinivasan. I told her that there isn't a book on business for those in their mid-teens and that I would love to write one someday—not a textbook but one that engages young readers just like fiction does, and yet opens their minds to the world of business that they tend to ignore but inevitably get impacted by. Sumitra promptly agreed that it would be great to have such a book. She told me that the Puffin editor, who would take the idea forward, is Sudeshna Shome Ghosh. Sudeshna happened to be the commissioning editor for my very first book, *The High Performance Entrepreneur*.

In December 2008, Sudeshna drew up a contract and that was the beginning of my woes. Now it was no longer an idea; I had to write the book! It was a difficult time for me because I was busy with my third book, *The Professional*, and then its revised international edition that consumed all my spare time; on top of that, I have a day job at MindTree. As a result, despite my initial enthusiasm, for all of 2009 and 2010, I could produce nothing. In 2010, I managed to write half the book but, along the way, I realized that I was making a fundamental mistake. For over a decade, I had not interacted with anyone in their mid-teens! And that was my target group. The last teenager to leave home was our younger daughter Niti, way back in 2001. Before anything else, I needed to find out, first-hand, who today's sixteen-year-old is, what he or she wants to know about the world of business, what are his or her priorities and prejudices?

That is when I met Dr K.P. Gopalakrishna, founder of the National Public School group of educational institutions, and Dr Bindu Hari, Director of The International School Bangalore. I asked them if they would let me into the world of a bunch of sixteen-year-olds and allow me to work with them over several weekends to discuss the world of business. In the process, I would get to understand what goes on inside their minds and, hopefully, they would benefit too. The result was a programme we titled 'Business with Bagchi'. Over four weekends in January 2011, I worked with thirty-one amazingly bright young students who greatly impacted on how the book was written. The content was, indeed, determined by them. This book contains what they wanted to know and which, I presume, several sixteen-year-olds would want to know. Interacting with them also catalysed the single most important decision in the evolution of this book, as distinct from the initial idea—I trashed the old manuscript. At the end of our intense classroom and off-classroom interactions, I wanted to write a very different book. I hope that the way it has finally turned out will engage you.

I must acknowledge the contributions of many people who made this book possible.

I am immensely grateful to Sumitra and Sudeshna to start with, especially Sudeshna, for being patient with me for the three years I took to write a commissioned book and then editing it for me. I owe a huge debt of gratitude to Dr Gopalakrishna and Dr Bindu Hari who let me use their school as a laboratory. Mrs Shantha Chandran and Mrs Chitra Rao—the principals of National Public School's Indira Nagar and HSR Layout branch, respectively—and Mrs Lakshmi Rao, the vice-principal of NPS's Koramangala branch—took upon themselves the student selection process, the logistics and facilitation of parental consent. Chitra Rao hosted the four Saturday sessions and her staff members rearranged classrooms, got the pizzas and the colas and did everything possible to make me feel at home. To all these 'Ma'ams', I bow.

When 'Business with Bagchi' was announced, the aspirants were required to write a short essay on themselves as to who they were and their expectations. These were fed into analytics software by MindTree colleagues Ramanathan Gopalakrishnan and Lakshmi

Pawar. From the analysis emerged some fascinating data on the profile of today's sixteen-year-old. This was invaluable for me for my subsequent fruitful engagement with the group of thirty-one.

As 'Business with Bagchi' unfolded, I invited Harish Hande, the founder of SELCO India, to interact with the students. Six months after the momentous session with Harish, he went on to win the 2011 Ramon Magsaysay Award. Harish, thank you for your participation.

During the process of writing the book, one of my favourite sixteen-year-olds, Megha Harish, agreed to be my teen editor. She scrutinized the manuscript to vouch for content appropriateness and readability. Based on her suggestion, I made some really significant changes. Thank you, Megha, for making sure the book is 'teen tested'.

This is my fourth book and I had the most fun writing this one. Hopefully, as you read it, you will figure out why. The experience was like walking a high wire—I had to constantly keep in mind the all-important need to balance. I was fortunate to have known two wonderful people who provided unstinted support in this aspect. One is Lubna Kably, who I have known for many years, and the other is Manoj Karanth, my colleague at MindTree.

Sourav Mukherjee, one of my favourite teachers at the Indian Institute of Management, Bangalore, agreed to read the manuscript to certify if indeed it could be recommended reading for 'Teen MBA'. He has given a clean chit on that one, and I thank him for his time and encouragement.

Once the manuscript was in place, Geetha Mani Chandar, my irrationally reverent reader, ran it through a fine-tooth comb. Any and all inconsistencies you may subsequently find are attributable to her indulgence ☺.

In the end, my administrator Shanti Uday put the finishing touches so the manuscript could get the final okay from Sohini Mitra and Udayan Mitra at Penguin. To all of them, I am indebted.

Special thanks are due to Akira, the golden retriever in real life, who has acted as Cyber in chapter 9, and to my photographer friend Mallik Katakol, who indulged me through the making of this book.

Last, but not the least, I am grateful to each one of the thirty-one bright young people whose names are acknowledged in the dedication page. To all of them, I only have this to say: 'In letting me into your world, you made me feel sixteen all over again. May you become all that you dream of today and may you build the future that others will live!'

Subroto Bagchi
1 January 2012

Dedication

For the thirty-one boys and girls who worked with me during 'Business with Bagchi'; you made me feel that I was attempting something worthwhile.

Sidharth Sadrangani	Samvartika Bajpai	Aathira Sethumadhavan
Pragya Gupta	Adithya H.C.	Megha Harish
Jayatheerth S.	Aditya Roy	Kartik Agarwal
Karan Padgaonkar	Akshay Nelakruti	Naren Subbiah
Tanmay Sahay	Kamya Swaminathan	Sadhana Sanjay
Sowmya Khandelwal	Manisha Krishnan	Vikram Singh
Suheil Daryanani	Monica Sadhu	Aditi Chalisgaonkar

Aradhana C.V.	Pallavi Varma	Anvitha Prashanth
Nivrith Sekhar	Ragini R.	Siddharth Ramachandran
Sanket Shah	Rohit Pattanaik	Ashwin K.P.
Suprotik Das		

As you read this book, you will meet them all. In the chapters that follow, these young men and women appear as characters, though the situations, contexts and conversations are fictitious. So most of my characters bear resemblance to real people but not to what they do in this book! Also, other than Dr Gopalakrishna, Dr Bindu Hari and Principal Chitra Rao, all other teachers and staff members are figments of my imagination and bear no resemblance to people, dead or living.

With all that taken care of, shall we begin now with the real stuff?

Introduction

What Will I Be when I Grow Up?

As a little boy, I grew up in small places in tribal districts of eastern India. My earliest recollection of the world around me is from a place called Koraput. It was one of the most backward yet one of the most picturesque places, home to tribal people who grew paddy and millet, raised chickens and collected forest produce like firewood, fruit and berries. They brought these to the nearby town once a week and traded for kerosene, rice, sugar or salt from small-time traders who brought the merchandise from faraway places by train and bus.

By the time we came to Koraput, I was about five years old. I did not attend school because the nearest primary school was far away. I was taught at home by my parents. But my elder brother Aurobinda went to a school a few miles from home because he was old enough to walk the distance. One summer, when the family sat around in a circle on the floor in my mother's kitchen for the afternoon tea, he was asked what he wanted to be when he grew up. What he said shocked everyone.

'When I grow up, I want to be Somalingam,' he said.

***

Somalingam was the only grocer in the small town. In his hole-in-the-wall store, he stacked sacks of rice, wheat, sugar and tins of cooking oil and kerosene. Everyone shopped at his store because he sold on credit. Government officials could pay him only after they got their salaries at the end of the month; but once a week they sent their children or went themselves with large shopping bags and empty tins. Somalingam, a middle-aged man with no real education but a great ability to keep accounts, noted who owed him how much. Somalingam was always there in his shop; he took orders from his customers and yelled them out to someone at the back of the store. He had a couple of helpers, who seemed to be permanently bent at their backs, carrying sacks, stacking things neatly and extracting small quantities of whatever people asked for. Somalingam weighed the merchandise and poured them into the bag and tins as his customers waited patiently. Sundays were particularly busy as were the first few days of the month when everyone came to pay him his dues.

Coming from an educated, middle-class family, Aurobinda was expected to say that he wanted to become a doctor, an engineer, a teacher, join the army or work for the government. He could not become Somalingam! Heavens, no!

Somalingam was a businessman, a trader. And in families like ours, where no one understood the world of business, his ilk was looked down upon. Somalingam, it was suspected, hoarded sugar and kerosene in his godown and either sold them in times of scarcity to his favourite customers or charged unduly for them.

Decades later, the family was relieved that my brother became an army officer. Not a businessman. Coming from such a family, when I grew up, the alternatives suggested to me were diplomat, professor, civil servant or doctor. But, as things turned out, I ended up in the world of business. In the process, over the years, I learnt about how much we all depend on businesses of all kinds to be able to live comfortable lives, to do the things that make us happy every day. But it was not a matter of an informed career choice. Today, in a world of global business in which roses from Bangalore reach Holland the next morning and Washington apples get sold in India, where goods and services move across the world, even small-town traders like sweaty Somalingam, who kept his accounts in a small diary, have mobile phones and Internet access. But something has not quite changed. Many families still do not understand how business works. As a result, many young adults are as unfamiliar with the world of business as the Bagchi household in the 1950s.

So I thought I should write this book for you young adults, future chief executives, founders of businesses, inventors whose path-breaking work will be converted into useful drugs and brought to the world by corporations. You are so important to our future that even though you may not need to make up your minds today about who you want to be, you do need to know about how business, trade and industry work. Even if you do not want to study for a master's in business management (MBA), become a chief executive officer (CEO) or start your own company, the world of business touches everyone's lives. It helps to know.

To be able to write a book like this, I needed some serious help from sixteen-year-old folks. I needed to look at how they looked at the world of business, what intrigued them, what fascinated them and what worried them. Only then could I write something that young people like you may find worth their while. So I went to Bangalore's National Public School and asked them to lend me a bunch of sixteen-year-olds. The idea was to explore their minds as we together explored the world of business. A group of thirty-one bright young boys and girls worked with me over four weekends. They defined what they wanted to learn about business. They diligently maintained learning diaries after every session and returned with loads of questions that sometimes made me scamper for help. Together we watched business films, read case studies and articles and books; they made presentations and I listened intently; and I spoke while they took copious notes and, of course, we ate some pizza along the way. Then I sat down to write what finally is in your hands. I hope you will enjoy *MBA at* 16 and, in the process, learn some things interesting and useful about the world of business.

When you read this book, do not expect a conventional textbook that may help you improve your grades. It is no more a textbook on business than a Harry Potter book is on sorcery! But, like Harry Potter, I hope to fascinate you and draw you into another magical world from where you will return informed and inquisitive to explore more in the years to come. Each chapter in this book is a journey led by one or more of the thirty-one students I had the privilege of knowing. All you have to do is to let them lead the way and you just go along.

CHAPTER 1

One Day in the Life of Manisha Krishnan

Manisha hated getting out of bed in the morning. Why must school start so early and why must she be up by 6 a.m.? It was a tussle every day. First mom and then dad had to cajole, pester, and yell before she finally got up.

One day, she produced convincing proof of why it is natural for young adults like her to sleep late—it is because of complex hormonal changes that make them 'naturally' want to stay awake late at night and sleep late into the day. Unimpressed with her discovery, her father growled that she better be ready in time for him to drop her to school the next day or else walk herself to school!

This morning, as she stumbled into the bathroom with bleary eyes, she couldn't care less about the toothbrush and toothpaste she was about to use. She had no clue that her Oral-B toothbrush was first designed by a California dentist named Dr Robert Hutson, who created it in 1950 and named it Oral-B 60, as it had sixty nylon bristles. The Oral-B 60 was on the moon mission aboard the *Apollo 11*. In any case, toothbrushes came into being only in 1938, once DuPont's scientists created nylon. Before that, people in India used twigs and, in the US and elsewhere, animal hair! Eww! She didn't need to know that.

* * *

Manisha emerged from the bathroom, looking squeaky-clean and set for the day. The shower made all the difference. After donning her school uniform that she so loved to hate, she inspected her face in the mirror. Like all teenagers, she was unsure whether she looked pretty or horrible. Strange, how she alternated between extremes. This morning, she chose pretty because they had dramatics rehearsal after school and the very thought put a spring in her step. Her mood magically lifted and she was rather sweet to her mother as she reported for breakfast.

She liked Kellogg's cereals for breakfast. It was the quick and easy way to gulp down stuff, unlike the weekend when she rustled up her own omelette. As she unmindfully gobbled her cereal, she read the comics section of the newspaper.

Usually her father would growl, 'You must read the front page first!' He always sounded as if he were speaking from a pulpit. She would say, 'Yes, yes,' and stick to Calvin and Hobbes.

The cornflakes she ate this morning came from corn grown a thousand miles away. Kellogg's purchased the corn from the farmers and brought them to their factory, where the corn on the cob became cornflakes in the carton.

Can you imagine, in 2010, Kellogg's was a 12-billion-dollar global company by simply serving cereals of all types!

Kellogg's was started by a man named Will Keith Kellogg, who had studied up to sixth grade, and his brother Dr John Harvey Kellogg. They were Seventh-Day Adventists, managing a sanatorium in the US and looking to provide a vegetarian diet for the inmates. By accident, in trying to save some boiled wheat one day, they put it under a roller, expecting dough. Instead, they got flakes. When they roasted the flakes and fed them to their patients, they simply loved it! Encouraged, the brothers experimented with corn and that is how cornflakes were first created. They applied for a patent on 31 May 1895, and so the journey began.

Engrossed in Calvin and Hobbes, Manisha was quite unmindful of the fact that her father was already in the car downstairs, waiting for her. When her mother warned her that he would soon fidget and rant, she jumped off her chair, gathered her school bag, left the newspaper in a big mess on the dining table and scampered down.

Manisha only looked forward to the comics section of the newspaper every morning—somehow she never thought of the newspaper as a business. She did not really stop to think that the newspaper industry was indeed a large business that employed thousands of people who gathered, edited, composed and printed the pages at night while the world slept. The papers were then carried all over the country by plane, train and bus, segregated at street corners early next morning by hawkers who then went house to house, distributing them. The newspaper business earned money by selling not just subscriptions, but by collecting advertising revenue. Even in India, where 35 per cent of the 1.2 billion citizens cannot read or write, there are over 62,000 newspapers of all kinds in circulation. Though every major paper can be read online, people still prefer the printed paper delivered at home, which implies the global consumption of millions of metric tonnes of newsprint every year!

* * *

Manisha's father dropped her to school and drove off. As she ran in, she did not stop to think that education itself could be a business. She would, of course, hate to think of it that way. How could a school be a business? The fact, however, is that school and college fees, sales of books and other teaching aids, tests like GRE and TOEFL, all these add up to a neat pile. Countries like England and Australia see themselves as education destinations and actively promote education as an industry.

The amount of money spent on education is indeed staggering. In India, states like Tamil Nadu, Karnataka,

Maharashtra and Odisha are turning out to be centres of higher education; students spend enormous amounts of money to get admitted into private schools and professional colleges in these states. Though estimates vary, the education business in India alone is in excess of 42 billion dollars annually and is predicted to grow at 15 per cent every year for the next five years.

* * *

School was great fun today. They had a couple of tests, the usual lectures including her dreaded chemistry class, a round of basketball during recess but the crowning glory was the play rehearsal. For weeks, the class had been practising for an inter-school competition being held by a leading newspaper that believed in catching them young. By the time Manisha got home, it was evening. She kicked off her shoes, peeled off her smelly socks and crashed on her bed for a much-needed siesta before she started her second shift.

If it weren't for Mrs Krishnan every day, Manisha would sleep through to the morning. Today was different. Even before her mother came in to switch on the lights, she got up on her own, feeling famished. She went to the kitchen, opened the refrigerator and surveyed the leftovers. She was her Mom's clean-up crew. She saw Maggi noodles from yesterday, a wedge of tiramisu and a pear.

Pear was her favourite fruit. The one sitting on her plate this evening was actually grown in China. Only a week ago was it plucked, boxed and shipped a few thousand miles from Dalian. India has now opened her markets to fruits and vegetables that come all the way from China, Australia and the US, just as these countries allowed Indian agricultural produce to be sold in their markets under bilateral treaties.

After her snack, Manisha opened her computer and soon her fingers were flying over the keyboard as she simultaneously chatted with her friends Aditya and Kamya, updated her Facebook account about an impending field trip to Chikmagalur that was now on and now off for some time, and then she downloaded some music from her favourite website. In the process, she used a Dell computer, a Cisco router and an Internet service provided by Airtel—of course, all paid for by her parents.

She could not wait until the day she could pay for and get stuff from the Internet using her own account and her very own credit card. But that was still a few years away! Meanwhile, she and her friends at National Public School (NPS) were grateful for their Gmail accounts and their world of YouTube, Facebook, Twitter and all things free. Manisha was pretty curious about entrepreneurs who set up these companies. Her friend Karan was a storehouse of information on their fascinating stories of innovation and grit.

At about 8 p.m., Manisha shut the computer down and sat at her desk to do her homework. By 10 p.m., she would have dinner with her parents and her younger sister and then work for another couple of hours. She would hit the sack well past midnight.

Manisha Krishnan had no idea how many businesses had touched her from the time she opened her eyes in the morning to the time she was ready to dream, secure in the knowledge that she was in her own bed, in the comfort of her own home.

Speaking of home, she lives with her parents in a nice neighbourhood quite close to her school. Her parents raised a bank loan to purchase the house a few months ago. Though it feels really nice to live in a house of her own, Manisha seldom looks at it as something that several businesses had converged to create.

For instance, the construction company that had sold the house to her parents had bought cement and steel, hollow bricks and ceramic fittings, floor tiles and electrical appliances and many other things that were, in turn, manufactured and sold by a host of other companies. The construction company had also purchased the land, hired the services of an architect to design the entire apartment complex and finally put the housing project together. Each player in the orchestration is a business. In turn, each one buys raw material from a host of suppliers, moves manufactured goods from a factory to a warehouse to a shop before the housing company buys them all, builds a house and then delivers it to folks like the Krishnans.

Since Manisha's parents did not have all the money they needed to pay for the house right up-front, they went to a bank and availed of a housing loan. Housing loans are usually long-term loans that people repay over five, ten, even twenty years. Banks that lend money for housing require the house to be pledged as a security; it is an assurance or a guarantee that the money loaned would come back to the bank with the agreed interest. The property is thus 'mortgaged' to the bank until the loan is repaid in full. The idea is that the bank can take over the house if the borrower fails to pay up.

India's housing needs have been growing at an astounding rate—there is a shortfall of 16.53 million dwelling units according to one estimate; billions of dollars of international investment are flowing in to meet the demand and the housing sector has witnessed 22 per cent compounded annual growth in recent years. But tonight, Manisha must sleep—oblivious to the myriad ways in which the world of business cocoons her so that she can attend school, grow up, find work one day, create her own nest and play her part in the world she will call her own.

CHAPTER 2

The Happy School Bus

The excitement among the students of NPS was palpable. Their field trip to Chikmagalur, which nearly got cancelled due to non-availability of the commerce teacher, Mr Ramesh Ramanathan, was finally cleared. The computer science teacher, Mrs Pratima Rao—nicknamed Prat Rao—had agreed to take the students for the trip away from Bangalore, over to the hills of Chikmagalur, to a coffee plantation, where they could study a real-life enterprise and use the visit to understand the profiles of people who set up business ventures. In the process, they were to get a feel of what makes an entrepreneur different from other people. A few weeks before the trip, the group had researched a few companies and their founders on their own. It was agreed that during the field trip, the students would make presentations on their learning as well.

Everyone was delighted with the substitution of Prat Rao in place of Mr Ramanathan. Not that Mr Ramanathan was bad, just that he was way too serious. The man never smiled. He had a forbidding look though he was pretty harmless. In contrast, Prat Rao was immensely popular with all the students. She was really good at her own subject, and, more important, she looked ten years younger than she was. She treated the students in class ten and above like friends and that made her really cool. With Prat Rao around, there would be no lecturing, no admonishing looks, no checking on which boy sat next to which girl and, probably, no boring instructions. Karan was the first one to find out and immediately tweeted it. Within minutes, all of them had the good news.

Winter break commenced from Monday and the trip was to start on Friday evening. On Friday, after school, the students were to leave in a bus from school, snaking out of Bangalore's chaotic traffic, hitting the national highway to Hassan, turning off to Chikmagalur via Belur and then slowly ascending into the verdant hills of the Western Ghats to reach the Devadarshini Estate, where they would stay overnight in tented accommodation provided by their gracious hosts Café Coffee Day. The next day would bring a trip to one of their coffee estates, with insights into coffee cultivation, curing and understanding the process from bean to brew. On Sunday, the students were required to discuss what they had learnt, in small groups, followed by a paper presentation on the lives of some entrepreneurs they truly admired. On Monday, the bus would take them to visit the twelfth century ruins of Belur and Halebidu and they would return to Bangalore the next day.

Everyone was super excited. During recess, Pallavi, Ragini and Manisha sat together with their lunches, like always, to discuss what to pack and what music to carry for the road. True, it was a trip arranged to study how businesses worked and what entrepreneurs were like, but the sheer idea of getting away from home and routine, and that too with friends, made everyone agog with anticipation. Pallavi and Ragini were the ones more interested in the world of business; to Manisha, business was just another thing. She was not opinionated, unlike many young people. For now, she was signed up and happy about the trip, even though it was still a few days away.

Like her, the thirty other students, lost in the sheer thrill of a getaway, had no idea where the trip would finally take them.

* * *

Finally it was Friday afternoon. The brand new bus designated for the trip pulled up in front of the school gate. The effect was electric. 'Come on, come on everyone, we don't want to reach very late,' Prat Rao tried to raise her voice above the din. The excited boys and girls were clambering all over like puppies let loose on a spring day. Some were reaching out for the best seats by the window, some were clamouring for overhead space for their backpacks. A bunch was busy taking pictures in front of the bus and, since they did not trust the driver's photography skills, it was quite a long process. But Prat Rao called the bunch to order, took a headcount, nodded to the driver Raju and the bus rolled out, with a loud 'yay' from the students.

Mercifully, it wasn't rush hour and the bus soon hit the national highway towards Hassan, which has India's largest satellite tracking station. From there, they would turn towards Belur, home to the 1,000-year-old Chennakesava Temple and continue towards Chikmagalur city and then climb the hills, verdant with thousands of acres of coffee. The first hour was cacophonous—MP3 players changed hands, there was some verbal sparring, a few songs were sung, Prat Rao pretended to yell at some kids as lots of chips and drinks were passed around. Somewhere after the small town of Kunigal, the passengers suddenly became very quiet. Most of the students slept off; a few relished the beautiful, green world outside: the faraway hills, a sudden patch of sunflowers and, far out there where the sky and the earth met, a gentle indication that dusk was due. When the bus finally turned towards Belur, a little before Hassan, the travellers stirred back to life. That meant a bio-break and more snacks, and soon they were back on to a narrower but rather nicely maintained road. Only when the bus crossed Chikmagalur and started climbing could one make out the coffee estates in the headlights, particularly at bends. Everyone could see the dark-leaved shrubs amidst the taller trees like silver oak, orange and jackfruit and black pepper vines climbing on any willing host. By the time they reached Devadarshini Estate, they were all pretty tired. The bus pulled into what looked like a nice old bungalow from yore. The group was received by a very warm and friendly gentleman called Javed. He was the estate manager. He told everyone to eat dinner and sleep early so that the next morning they could explore the estate and learn about the business right after breakfast.

'Listen everyone,' Prat Rao announced, 'finish breakfast and assemble here sharp at 9 a.m., okay?'

'Okay Ma'am,' the group chorused and rushed towards the food.

* * *

Story has it that a Baba Budan from Chikmagalur went to Mecca on a pilgrimage way back in the 1600s. There he met Arab traders returning from Africa, and they gave him a few coffee beans. He brought back seven seeds, which he gave to his followers to cultivate. The beans got scattered about the hills that were home to Baba Budan and, in time, the locals discovered and cherished what came to be known as the Arabica Indica variety of coffee. Today, centuries later, Baba Budan's legacy has grown and, in 2009–10, India produced 2,89,000 tonnes of coffee, most of which found its way out of India.

The largest among all the coffee growers in India today is a man named V.G. Siddhartha. Siddhartha was born in a traditional coffee plantation family in Chikmagalur. The family had grown coffee for generations but did not have huge ambitions—they were content with a few hundred acres under cultivation. Siddhartha, the only son of his parents, finished studying economics and wanted to see the world for himself. He told his father that he wanted to learn about the world of financial investments; he wanted to go to faraway Mumbai and learn from a man named Mahendra Kampani whom he had never met. With permission from his father, young Siddhartha boarded a bus to Mumbai, where he rented a hotel room with a shared toilet.

Mumbai stunned Siddhartha—it was beyond his imagination. The next day, he went to see the man who was to become his mentor. At Kampani's high-rise office, he saw people waiting for the elevators at the ground level; he had never seen an elevator and was very self-conscious about riding one. He chose to climb the several floors instead and managed to meet Kampani. He talked himself into an apprenticeship and started working long days and late evenings under the tutelage of the famous investment manager and former president of the Bombay Stock Exchange. After nearly two years, when Siddhartha felt he had a good understanding of the world of money, he returned home to fully engage himself with the coffee business.

The coffee business was a difficult one. Estate owners found it challenging to manage alternating years of famine and glut. Siddhartha started buying the estates that were going out of business and revived them. Over time, the cultivation grew but he found himself at the mercy of international coffee bean buyers who had an upper hand in deciding coffee bean prices. So, rather than constantly having to negotiate for better prices, he decided to start his own chain to retail coffee. He shifted from selling the beans to selling the brew. That is how Café Coffee Day came into being. Today, the familiar cheery red sign dots thousands of places in the country.

Not only does Siddhartha sell coffee there but eatables as well because young people like to sit down and spend time over a sandwich and a piece of cake with their coffee. This was a classic case of the power of adjacency in the market. If you sell coffee, adjacent to it is the idea of a sandwich and also bottled water. But coffee retailing to selling sandwiches is not just about the food and the espresso machines; it is about people. Siddhartha needed thousands of trained young people to deliver the Café Coffee Day experience. Towards this, he opened a hospitality training institute in Chikmagalur, and another in Chennai, where he offered stipends to rural youth who could get trained for six months and then join the workforce. He thereby created thousands of jobs for people who otherwise would have found it difficult to compete in a rapidly growing but predominantly urban economy. In 2010, Siddhartha bought out Emporio, a coffee chain in the Czech Republic. That year, he had a sales turnover of 100 million dollars, serving more than one million cups of coffee a day!

Siddhartha's decision to move from selling coffee beans to retailing the brew was non-trivial. When someone shifts from selling a raw material to a finished product, it is called moving up the value chain. Each point of transition, from bean to the hot cup of coffee, is a point of added value. If you sell coffee beans in gunny bags, you make some money. Roast the bean and crush it, package it in tins and sell through grocery stores, your profit margins go up. Convert that into cups of coffee served in a pleasant setting, the profitability surges further. As do the complexities. The complexity may involve learning a whole new set of things that a coffee plantation owner does not know. Think of logistics, for instance. How do you make sure that thousands of stores are stocked with the right inventory when customers walk in? How do you choose the store locations right and make the right commercial deals? How do you recruit, train and retain a motivated crew? When an entrepreneur takes on all these additional dimensions, there are inherent risks that must be managed so that eventually the rewards may follow.

* * *

After spending a fantastic day in the coffee estate and learning all about Baba Budan and Siddhartha, the group met Javed in the evening. A nice campfire was blazing and hot soup was served. Javed was bombarded with many questions from the eager group. They asked about how he measures productivity, some asked about sustainable plantation practices, a few students wanted to know what it was like to work for Siddhartha and what did he review when he came by. Javed was happy and patiently answered all their questions. Prat Rao listened to the lively conversation and sometimes chimed in with her editorial comments. Everyone admired how well versed she was in so many different things and not just pigeonholed in her own subject.

A few weeks before the group had set out on the field trip, some of the students had volunteered to research Biocon, the iconic biotech company set up by Kiran Mazumdar Shaw. Before everyone got up from the still lingering embers of the campfire, Prat Rao announced that they would share their findings with the larger group after breakfast the next day.

When Prat Rao came out from her room the next morning, the students were already up and ready. She looked younger in her jeans and smart shirt which did not escape the attention of her brood. But they all chorused, 'Good morning, Ma'am,' and then everyone settled down to a sumptuous breakfast. After breakfast, Prat Rao herded them all to the lawn where chairs had been arranged and a flip-chart board organized.

'Who is presenting?' Prat Rao asked. Aradhana and Nivrith stepped forward. 'Sit down everyone, let us start,' she instructed. The presentation began.

***

While the story of Café Coffee Day was about agri-business to retail, Biocon was about the intersection of advanced scientific research and the steely determination of one woman who wanted to prove that you can do it, if you really wanted to.

In 2010, *Time* magazine named Biocon's founder-chairperson Kiran Mazumdar Shaw among the world's most influential people, for her work in the area of cancer research. Biocon and its sister concerns were together at the forefront of India's biotech revolution, working in a variety of fields like drug discovery, production of oral insulin and contract research on behalf of other companies. Kiran's father was a brewer by profession, working for companies in the alcohol business. As a young adult, Kiran wanted to be a doctor but narrowly missed the qualifying mark. She could have studied medicine and qualified as a doctor if her father had agreed to pay a rather large 'donation' to a medical college. It was and is a common practice in India. Her father refused. Kiran tugged at parental emotion by asking him to pay the donation or the 'capitation fee', as it is called, instead of saving up for her wedding. Mazumdar Senior was undeterred. Kiran was heartbroken but she learnt a key lesson—to earn her place by dint of merit. She signed up for zoology instead and subsequently decided to become India's first qualified woman brewer. She went to Australia to study brewing.

After excelling in her studies, she returned to India. She was in for a second disappointment. No one would give her a job! Brewing was a male bastion. While she was still looking around, a mutual friend introduced her to an Irish company named Biocon that was looking for an Indian partner to make enzymes out of papaya. With all of 10,000 rupees, she started the venture virtually in a garage. The business took off; soon she was making a host of enzymes. Think of an enzyme as the yeast we use at home to make yoghurt or bake bread. Similarly, cultured enzymes are used for many different applications, from making beer to providing a certain texture to clothes people wear and so on. After becoming very successful at this, Kiran set her sights higher. She was no longer content making enzymes—she wanted to build drug molecules. She was concerned that diseases like diabetes were so prevalent in a highly populated country like India. India needed low-cost, easy-to-administer medicines. Many people, including one of her key customers and an investor, discouraged her but she persisted. Biocon started work on an oral insulin and other drugs and eventually sold off its enzyme business to fully focus on drug discovery and research. Today, Biocon employs 4,000 highly qualified scientists, researchers and production personnel who bring out a wide range of drugs and formulations, and is well on its way to becoming the first billion-dollar company from India in the biotechnology arena.

When Aradhana and Nivrith finished their presentation, everyone was very impressed. The group sat around and discussed many things, in particular the need for women entrepreneurs as role models in a country where 50% of the population consisted of women.

* * *

On Monday morning, the happy school bus was ready for its journey back. It was kind of sad that the group of thirty-one had to leave. The lovely treks in the coffee plantation dotted with bushes of red berries waiting to be plucked, the abundant vines of black pepper and vanilla, the sheer greenery of the rainforest with canopies of jackfruit and rosewood and orange and silver oaks, the gurgling streams that ran through the estates in abandon and, in the evenings, as the campfire became an ember, the startlit sky overhead with the song of a thousand grasshoppers in concert—all this was too much to leave behind.

With mixed feelings, the group herded back into the bus. Prat Rao knew how it felt because she too was sixteen one day! She got all of them together before it was time to board the bus and, to cheer them up, explained the wonderful day that lay ahead. The group was going to stop at the famous 10th century temple at Belur, and then visit the breathtaking ruins of the Hoysala Empire in Halebidu where time stood still. She told them about the fabled King Vishnuvardhana and his beautiful wife and how the great architecture they created fell to the advance of the invader Malik Kafur in the early part of the 14th century. Everyone listened to her in rapt attention and then, briefing over, thanked Javed and all the people who had taken care of them so well during the stay. On behalf of the class, Megha handed over a big box of chocolates to the staff of the Devadarshini Estate and said in Kannada, *tumba dhanyavada,* meaning, many thanks.

After their visit to Belur and then Halebidu, the group converged on one important decision: they would continue to pursue the fantastic world of business and entrepreneurship even as the field trip was getting over. It was too interesting to leave behind as a casual encounter. They decided that they would explore, learn and exchange ideas among themselves.

* * *

Back in Bangalore, everyone had to return to the world of four-walled classrooms and the demands of the CBSE syllabus, the mock tests, the extra classes, the weekend tuitions, the homework . . . Yet, amidst it all, something had changed forever. It was as if the group had discovered a whole new world out there that was as fascinating as anything else of serious interest to them. It is interesting how, once you become conscious of something, you begin to connect to information about it in inexplicable ways. You suddenly discover it in all the stuff that had always existed around you, but you never noticed. Now, from newspapers and television stories, from the business books that their parents brought home to blogs, the youngsters were absorbing stories, news, data, graphs and charts. Their Facebook posts and tweets and blogs had a whole new dimension. It was another kind of buzz. Interestingly, even their conversations with dads and moms acquired a charmingly different angle. Word spread to the students of many rival schools that something extraordinary was happening at NPS.

CHAPTER 3

Karan Padgaonkar Meets Steve Jobs

Karan Padgaonkar was studying commerce. After school, he wanted to study economics and read for an MBA, get some work experience and, eventually, build an enterprise. His idol was Steve Jobs, the legendary founder of Apple. Karan knew a lot about the history of Apple yet wondered what it took to build great companies like that. What were entrepreneurs made of? Every time he thought of qualities that made someone an entrepreneur, he thought of Steve Jobs.

During long summer afternoons, Karan's dad would chat to him about great businesspeople. That whetted his curiosity. One day, driving past a brand new Apple store in Jayanagar, Karan's dad told him that Steve was all of sixteen when he met his friend Stephen Wozniak, with whom he went on to build the multi-billion-dollar cult company. Wow! Karan was fascinated more than ever before. As he learnt more about Steve's early life, his respect and admiration grew manifold. Before that, he had presumed that people who created big businesses were inevitably born with a silver spoon or at least were destiny's favoured children. He imagined corporate jets, oak-panelled intrigue-filled boardrooms, power trips and billions strewn in their path—not of someone like Steve facing an existential fork, right at birth!

Steve was given up at birth for adoption by his single mother. His foster parents sent him to school and later on to college, but Steve dropped out. He attended courses in calligraphy instead. He travelled all the way to India in search of spiritual enlightenment and returned a Buddhist. In 1974, he took up the job of a technician at a video game company called Atari. During the course of his work and via his interest in electronics, he met the other founders of Apple. Between 1977—when the company was registered—and 1984, Apple had a dream run, introducing a whole range of personal computers that withstood competition from significantly larger computer companies of the day. In May 1985, Steve was thrown out of Apple by the board because of the differences in opinion he had with the CEO of the day, John Sculley, a man he himself had brought into Apple!

Steve became a refugee from Apple for the next eleven years and started his next company called Next, Inc. Though it made news, its high-end, over-engineered computers did not sell as well. But Steve persisted, shifting focus from hardware to software. Along the way, he bought Pixar, the animation company behind such films as *Monsters, Inc.*, *Finding Nemo*, *Ratatouille* and the *Toy Story* franchise. Eventually, Steve sold Pixar to Walt Disney for a whopping 7.4 billion dollars and became its largest shareholder at the same time.

In 1996, Steve returned to Apple. Under his leadership, Apple went way beyond just computers to introduce path-breaking products like the iPod, the iPhone and the iPad, which have transformed the way people experience, literally 'live,' technology.

Around the time Steve was getting to be famous in Silicon Valley, up north in Seattle, Washington, surrounded by beautiful green mountains and lakes, was growing up another young man who changed the way the world used computers. His name was Bill Gates.

* * *

The world of high-technology companies is rife with stories of rivalries between technologists and companies themselves. If someone is in the Apple camp, he is not supposed to like Microsoft. If someone likes Android phones, then the Apple iPhone is a non-starter for him. At times, the rivalries are pushed too far. One day, Karan asked his dad to compare Steve Jobs and Bill Gates. Who was the greater of the two titans? Somehow, admiring Bill seemed like blasphemy to Karan. But when he learnt about how Bill had built his own company, he realized that independent of technological loyalty, there is so much to admire the Microsoft founder for.

Bill Gates founded Microsoft along with his friend Paul Allen. He was born to well-to-do parents who wanted him to be a lawyer, but he chose to pursue other things like starting a two-man software company after dropping out of Harvard University at a time when no one knew software could even be branded and sold before going forward! When he was a student at the Lakeside School in Seattle, the Mother's Club there bought a 'teletype terminal' with the proceeds of a rummage sale. A teletype terminal was like a typewriter with a display strip somewhat like that of a large calculator. These were precursors to the display units of modern computers. Think of a teletype as a poor man's computer terminal. The mothers paid for computer time on a GE-owned computer so that students could play around with the teletype. It was a momentous move.

Bill and his friends started playing with the teletype terminal in school. Yes, playing! They wrote incipient programs using the BASIC language and played tic-tac-toe with the computer. That is how Bill Gates was initiated into the world of computing.

When children play with something and find it 'neat', as Bill found the GE computer, they want to play some more. But all play eventually must end, particularly when money runs out. So, when the funding got over, the GE timeshare arrangement ended. Bill and his friends started looking for other places to rent computer time from, and this brought them to a company named Computer Center Corporation. They found a bug in the computer's operating system and, through the bug, a way to extract free time on it. After all, boys will be boys! Before they could suck the juice out of the system, the company discovered the prank and threw the boys out. But it admired them enough to readmit them, once they agreed to debug the system. In lieu of free computer time, of course!

Finally, childhood over, Bill went to Harvard. It took him just one year to decide that college was not the place he wanted to be in at that time. He dropped out and went to Albuquerque to join his Lakeside buddy Paul. They started a company named Micro-Soft in 1975. A year later, the hyphen was dropped. Eventually, the two came to Bellevue in Seattle, Washington, to build the company that soon became a household name.

Initially, Microsoft was focused on building a BASIC interpreter and, then, a compiler. In 1980, IBM Corporation was working on the soon-to-be-launched IBM personal computer, for which they needed a BASIC compiler. As IBM was in conversation with Microsoft, Bill and Paul learnt that IBM also needed an operating system and its negotiations with a company named Digital Research were not getting anywhere. The two decided to seize the opportunity by buying an operating system called Q-DOS from another company and renaming it 86-DOS. They offered to license 86-DOS to IBM, and it became PC-DOS on IBM computers. Bill and his associates anticipated that there would be many others who would bring out personal computers similar to IBM. They foresaw the emergence of clones or IBM-PC look-alikes soon. So they did not give away all rights to their product on an exclusive basis to IBM while licensing PC-DOS. They retained the right to license it with variations to other PC makers. In the process, Microsoft's operating systems like MS-DOS and Windows and later variants became de facto standards.

Bill worked very hard. He defended his corporation against much criticism and many lawsuits, and pretty much remained the technology fountainhead as well as the CEO of the organization. Later, he hired his Harvard buddy Steve Ballmer to replace him at the top of Microsoft and devoted his time mostly to the Bill and Melinda Gates Foundation, which works to eradicate malaria and AIDS and brings education to the underprivileged people in Africa and Asia. As of 2011, it is said that Bill and his wife Melinda have already contributed 28 billion dollars in charity. Fascinating stories of entrepreneurship are not limited to the high-tech world or, for that matter, the West. India is a country of great entrepreneurs, starting from the legendary founder of the House of Tata, Sir Jamsetji Tata. Thanks to the liberalized economy via which India is fast becoming a part of global business, we are witnessing an unprecedented surge in entrepreneurship and transformation in social norms.

***

Enterprises created by the likes of Steve Jobs, Bill Gates, V.G. Siddhartha and Kiran Mazumdar Shaw exemplify what we call 'for-profit' businesses. The fundamental reason why people from Somalingam to Steve Jobs build businesses is to make money. It is a different story that many amongst such businessmen may not use the money for their personal gain alone—they create more businesses that usher in jobs, build valuable things for humanity and, at times, devote substantial personal wealth to social welfare.

As mentioned, all businesses so created were known as 'for-profit' businesses until recently. No one ever thought that there could also be something called 'not-for-profit business'. In the last couple of decades, we are witnessing a whole new class of enterprise, termed 'not-for-profit business' or social enterprise created by people who are called social entrepreneurs.

These are people who use all the principles of enterprise-building (and possess similar personal characteristics as entrepreneurs in 'for-profit' ventures) but create organizations to solve social problems and to uplift the lives of the poor and the underprivileged. They set up and run their organizations based on the idea of self-sufficiency, they generate money from their own incomes to support a cause rather than seek donations and aid. In short, they run their businesses with innovation and efficiency but do not take the profit out of the organization for personal need; the money earned is ploughed back to create larger good for society. More on that with Kamya Swaminathan.

CHAPTER 4

Kamya Goes Solar

Kamya Swaminathan's mother studied business and specialized in finance at Harvard. When the family returned to India, she did not want to work for the for-profit sector. She wanted to channelize her knowledge into addressing urgent social issues and chose to work with the Azim Premji Foundation. The family often got together to discuss interlinked social issues like poverty and education. 'The poor are poor because they are poor,' said her mom one day. Kamya was completely baffled.

She went on to explain the concept of the 'vicious cycle of poverty,' first propounded by economist E.F. Schumacher, who left a lasting impact on the world with his ideas on what the developing world really needed as against what the West propagated. Schumacher felt that efforts to alleviate poverty usually fail because the poor are always trapped in a vicious cycle. Consider this: A man is poor. So, he has no savings. Because he has no savings, he has no assets. Because he has no assets, he cannot offer collateral or a mortgage to get a bank loan. Because a bank will not give him a loan, he cannot start a business or improve his condition in any way. As a result, he stays poor. That was amazingly simple and explained why, for centuries, large parts of Asia, Africa and South America have remained in conditions of misery.

'So, to uplift someone from poverty, one has to break the vicious cycle at some point,' explained Kamya's mom. One way is for the poor people to form 'cooperatives', where a number of poor people come together to solve their own economic problems with small amounts of money. The cooperative movement actually spread quite a bit in the last century and that is how we saw the emergence of many significant cooperative efforts, some of which became hugely successful. One of them is India's White Revolution led by the legendary Verghese Kurien, who made Amul a household name via Operation Flood. The success of Amul transformed India from a milk-deficient country to a milk-surplus one, within the span of a generation. India's milk production was lagging behind demand because most households in the villages had only one cow or buffalo. They could not carry their meagre milk production to big cities and towns. So, they sold it to middlemen who swindled them. In came Kurien, who asked the individual producers to come together and form cooperatives—when a large number of milk farmers came together and collected their individual production in one place, suddenly it was not small any more. Individually, they were insignificant. Collectively, they were significant enough for a milk tanker to come all the way to their village and pick up the production, eliminating the middleman who not only exploited the villagers economically but also perpetrated other injustices. This story has been touchingly told by film-maker Shyam Benegal in *Manthan* ('The Churning'). So, when the villagers formed what came to be known as a milk cooperative, they could extend its power to strike bargains in buying everything, from their own day-to-day needs to fodder for their cattle. As a country, within decades, India transformed.

The cooperative movement transformed individuals, families and villages wherever it worked well. Not all cooperatives did. But, by and large, the idea of cooperatives worked for the poor but not for the poorest of the poor. They remained outside the boundaries of economic activity, trapping them in a state of endless misery. Until an economist named Mohammad Yunus arrived on the scene in Bangladesh, after its independence from Pakistan in 1971.

Yunus did not have to study economics to know poverty. He was born to a poor family, in a poor village, in a poor country. Despite the debilitating poverty and his mother's mental illness, the young Yunus pursued his education well enough to earn a Fulbright scholarship and get to the US. There he finished with a doctorate from Vanderbilt University and became an assistant professor at Middle Tennessee State University. He could have lived a comfortable American life but his call of duty came when Bangladesh broke away from Pakistan.

The war-ravaged country needed reconstruction and, at the behest of Professor Nurul Islam, another economist who headed Bangladesh's planning commission, Yunus returned to serve his motherland. He had worked as a research assistant with Islam before leaving for the US.

The return to the motherland was not easy. To begin with, Yunus found the government job boring. He quit and went back to teaching, this time at University of Chittagong. Shortly after, in 1974, Bangladesh witnessed a terrible famine. As things worsened, Yunus felt a deep inner compulsion to get involved. He was not a rich man who could solve the problem with money. He was an economist and he needed to fix the issue of economic deprivation at the level of an equation first.

According to him, the poor could not get access to capital because, over centuries, banking institutions had been trained to lend money in certain defined ways. They lent money to people who already had enough and could provide collaterals, because the lenders were always looking for safety. They tried to protect themselves via elaborate paperwork and lawyers. And they gave out large sums; they did not like to lend tiny amounts. The cost of managing debt via the required amount of paperwork and the cost of recovery remained the same whether you lent a hundred or a million. So, large banks liked large borrowers.

Poor people invariably needed tiny amounts at a time, enough to buy, say, a cartload of vegetables that they could sell over the next couple of days. They were not literate, so they had no use for paperwork and because they were poor, they could give no collateral. But they had honourable intentions—if someone was willing to loan them small amounts, they would put it to work, earn some more and return the principal with interest so that they could borrow some more when the need arose. Banks were not trained to deal with such people.

Yunus discovered another interesting thing, early in his experiment with what came to be known as micro-credit: this happened well before his Grameen Bank became a household name in Bangladesh. He found that when he loaned a small amount of money to a poor man and a similar amount to a poor woman, the woman was more likely to put the money to productive use and, as a result of that, return to repay the debt. In villages, the women had a stronger sense of responsibility for their families—the men did not care as much. They were more prone to blowing the money away and return to the vicious cycle of poverty.

So Yunus took out a small amount from his meagre personal resources and lent it in even smaller amounts to a group of women, and that is how the miracle of micro-credit was born. The women formed a support group, helping each other stay the course in putting the money to productive use. They earned some money by selling something or buying poultry or a cow or a goat that they could use as a regenerative source of income. They also introduced new members to the group, thereby providing personal guarantee for new borrowers. The money earned as interest was lent to these newer borrowers. The pool of money grew, the borrowers grew, they all started building thousands of small businesses and the idea led to the formation of the Grameen Bank.

Bangladesh is one of the world's poorest and most populous countries even today. Being poor in Bangladesh is not just about economics and politics but also about religion. Being an Islamic nation, clerics threatened the women borrowers that they would be refused a Muslim burial because borrowing and lending money for interest is prohibited in Islam. Yunus persisted in his efforts and, by 2007, Grameen Bank had lent a staggering 6.38 billion dollars to 7.4 million small borrowers. He and his people had developed Grameen Bank into a globally admired model of poverty alleviation by treating the poor with respect. In 2006, the Nobel Peace Prize was awarded jointly to Yunus and the Grameen Bank.

* * *

Just as Mohammad Yunus was quietly creating an economic miracle with the poor in Bangladesh with his social enterprise, in Tamil Nadu in India, a doctor named Govindappa Venkataswamy—better known as Dr V—was creating a miracle in healthcare through his social enterprise, Aravind Eye Hospital.

Dr V was born in Vadamalapuram village in Tamil Nadu in 1918 to a poor household. In a film titled *Infinite Vision*, he recounts how, as a child, he had to tend to the family buffalo every morning before heading to school. As a child, he once heard that a young woman in the village had died while delivering her baby. He decided to become a doctor and save people from such untimely deaths. He studied to be an obstetrician and joined the army. Fate had other designs though. He contracted a rare form of arthritis that caused his fingers and toes to get misshapen. The army let go of him. He could no longer do the work he was trained for. Undeterred, he retrained himself as an ophthalmologist and spent all his working life as an eye surgeon in Madurai. When he was fifty-eight, Dr V was asked to retire from his government service as per rules. Instead of taking it easy, Dr V decided to start an eleven-bed eye hospital with the avowed goal of fighting 'needless blindness'. India has the largest number of blind people in the world. In 1977, Dr V estimated the number at 12 million and, according to him, 80 per cent of it was needless because it was caused by cataract. Timely detection and surgical intervention could help people to lead normal, healthy lives. But in rural India, where most of these people lived, there was the terrible nexus of poverty, ignorance and, of course, lack of affordable healthcare cost was the biggest hurdle.

Dr V had great admiration for the fast food company McDonald's' business model, which had delivered billions of burgers across the world systematically, efficiently. When you produce things in high volume and at increased efficiency, you reduce costs and, thereby, unit prices. When prices come down, demand increases! That has been true of many things, from the personal computer to the cell phone to low-cost air travel and healthcare.

Dr V made the analogy that the sheer volume of eye patients in India meant that, with efficiency, it was possible to lower the cost per surgical procedure. And he did precisely that. Aravind Eye Hospital became the first hospital in the world to experiment with an assembly line approach to eye surgery. It used fixed assets like operating theatre and equipment on a three-shift basis so their utilization and, hence, recovery of fixed costs went up. Today, from an eleven-bed hospital, Aravind has spread into multiple facilities across India. In 2009, they treated 2.5 million people and conducted 3,00,000 operations. As many as two-thirds of all outpatients and three-fourths of all those operated upon did not have to pay anything!

One of the major causes of rural blindness is ignorance. Many people progressively lose sight because they do not know that their condition is treatable. Many do not have the means to undertake travel to a centre for treatment by themselves or may not have someone to take them there. For a person accompanying the patient, it means a loss of daily wage. So Aravind introduced buses that went from village to village with doctors who examined patients on site; the buses would then bring those requiring surgery to the centre and drop them back after recovery! Initially, Aravind had to import expensive intra-ocular lenses that were needed to restore normal vision after the surgery. Each cost over 100 dollars apiece. Over time, and with volumes, they could produce lenses themselves for less than 5 dollars apiece. Today, they actually export lenses!

* * *

'Has it ever occurred to you that it is the poor people in this world who live in greater darkness?' Kamya's mother asked her, as the two sat out in the balcony, looking at the city lights flickering on in the horizon. It was a magical moment and Kamya loved it—how the lights came on in ones and twos and you could count them and then they went viral and, before you knew it, the city was aglow, awash in a surreal luminosity.

'I know what you mean Ma. Illiteracy and poverty go hand in hand and, because of that, the poor who have no access to education get disenfranchised, are denied opportunities and live in a state of darkness of the mind.'

'No, not darkness of the mind but real darkness,' said Ma. Kamya couldn't comprehend her mother's thoughts but she realized that she was about to share something important. Kamya sat there, in the twilit balcony, waiting to be enlightened about real darkness.

Access to on-demand lighting is a privilege of position and power everywhere in the world. How much light you consume is dependent on how well off your parents are! A young man named Harish Hande realized this during his studies towards a doctorate at the University of Massachusetts in Boston, USA. That is how he eventually got interested in solar energy at that time. He had a chance to visit the Dominican Republic where, for the first time, he saw the connection between poverty and darkness. His heart bled and he decided to devote his life to bringing affordable energy to the poor. He then spent time in Sri Lanka, in a village where no one spoke English, to get a grip of rural needs and challenges. He developed solar solutions for the rural folk, not through the lens of the city dweller. For insance, he provided solutions for unusual needs like keeping rampaging elephants at bay! In the Srilankan village, the locals told him that the critical need was not heating or lighting but it was to keep elephants at bay, who came in herds at night, destroyed crops and huts and sometimes killed people. Harish created solar-charged electric fences to save life and property.

Eventually, he returned to India to set up SELCO, now a 4-million-dollar enterprise that continuously researches unique lighting applications to significantly improve the conditions of the rural and urban poor.

Consider a roadside vegetable vendor. The poor woman opens shop to catch the evening traffic, commuting home from work. Within a few hours, the place is engulfed in darkness and people do not stop by to shop for vegetables any longer. At times, her vegetables perish. Imagine her loss. Harish's team built a solar battery charging solution that created multiple economic opportunities. A man started the business of renting solar-charged car batteries. He loaded them in an autorickshaw every evening and rented the batteries for twenty-five rupees an evening to the vegetable sellers. When dusk fell, the solar lights came on, adding at least two business hours and facilitating significant economic benefits for the vendors. Every small entrepreneur's livelihood needs are unique. The needs of cobblers are different from, say, those of farmers. For each specific need, SELCO's Application R&D team builds a unique and affordable solution based on the principle that it must pay for itself and increase the earning potential of the user from the word go.

Harish could have taken up any lucrative job in a well-paying corporation anywhere in the world. Yet, despite great initial difficulty, with immense perseverance, he built his social enterprise to bring economic value to people who exist at the base of the economic pyramid.

His work requires that he spend most of his time in India. He has made a huge personal sacrifice to be where his work is—leaving his wife and two children in the US. He sees them for a few months every year but he feels that the poor and the needy customers of SELCO are his family as well. He has received several honours, including the United Nations Development Programme's Social Entrepreneur of the Year Award in 2007, and spoken about his work at global platforms such as the World Economic Forum in Davos, where leaders congregate annually to learn from each other and ascertain trends. In 2011, Harish was honoured with the prestigious Ramon Magsaysay Award.

From Steve Jobs to Harish Hande, from entrepreneurs who build for-profit companies to those who build social enterprises, there is a common streak. All these people are 'path creators.' Many of us can walk well when the path is shown, but very few can create a path where none exists. That is the stuff entrepreneurs are made of. Whether they are born with it or they acquire the ability as they go along, we really do not know.

The illuminated city of Bangalore no longer engaged Kamya's young mind. As she sat listening to her mother in rapt attention, she was thinking of the vast divide between the haves and the have-nots of the world and how one day she had to make her bit.

CHAPTER 5

Dr G. Meets His Match

Dr G., the founder of NPS, is not a man who is easily impressed. He was always known to have an uncanny ability to sift the grain from the chaff in a jiffy. An old-school educator, he had painstakingly created the now fifty-year-old institution, and concepts bandied about in the name of modern educational methods did not pass muster with him. Which is why his chance meeting with Prat Rao, a few weeks after the famous field trip, was laced with mild cynicism. They met in the school foyer and Dr G. asked if the 'picnic' was a good one. Prat Rao could have ignored the comment but she was proud of how much her brood had accomplished during the short trip and, more important, how they had since been following up on their own to build on their knowledge. So she politely countered the founder chairman's dig by saying that it was an unprecedented learning experience even for her. And then she threw in a minor challenge: 'Sir, you will be very surprised by the students. It is as if they have got a lesson in entrepreneurship, a lesson that could be the envy of MBA students.' Dr G. loved to be challenged. He looked at Prat Rao with respect and suggested that the boys and girls put up a presentation to him on the qualities of an entrepreneur by analysing some of the best in town. The gauntlet was thrown. The date was set, for two days later.

That was it. When Prat Rao told the students about the challenge, frantic activity ensued. As if bound together by some super intelligence, the group quickly made a shortlist of tasks. They divided the production work among themselves and agreed that they would showcase their knowledge based on the field trip, but expand the scope substantially to show that the trip had indeed helped them to analyse the idea of entrepreneurship in general. So, they would pick up a wider set of names, ten in all, and the names had to be representative in every way. They would zero in on people and ideas, large companies and small, men and women, products and services, and show Dr G. their true colours. Five individual posters were to be created. In each, two entrepreneurs would be presented. Each poster would be explained by a team of two students.

Day after came sooner than expected. The students had prepared well, yet everyone had butterflies in the stomach, knowing Dr G. would be a difficult customer.

They put up their posters in the library and soon Dr G. was duly escorted in by Prat Rao to a chorus of 'good afternoon, sir'. Dr G. customarily ignored it, looked around and announced, 'Let us begin!'

Aradhana C.V. and Nivrith Sekhar presented the first poster: 'We would like to discuss two great entrepreneurs of the state, a man and a woman, one who added new value and dimension to a traditional family business and another who started a cutting-edge technology business as a first-generation entrepreneur. We are talking about V.G. Siddhartha of Café Coffee Day and Kiran Mazumdar Shaw of Biocon. We believe that these two individuals exemplify two critical aspects of enterprise creation—the power of vision and the power of displacement. Vision is about the power to imagine a future that does not exist and then working, not in a present forward, but in a future backward manner. When Siddhartha thought about creating branded coffee outlets, none had ever existed in India. He was discouraged by experts and had no past data to turn to for inspiration. Actually, everyone said coffee consumption in India was going down and retailing coffee would not work. He went against the flow, contrary to popular wisdom. What he was able to see, people did not. In his vision, it was not about just coffee. It was about creating community spaces for young people. Kiran Mazumdar Shaw, on the other hand, saw a future in new drug research and has become a world leader in oral insulin. When she started off, her company was making enzymes. She could have been content with that. But she envisioned a different future. She wanted to make drugs. Why? She saw the population boom in India coming, making

India the disease capital of the world. That is how she thought of low-cost oral insulin for diabetes. Let us now look at the other critical aspect, that of displacement. We believe that all displacement is good, but most of us feel insecure about the idea whereas entrepreneurs show that displacement is elemental. Without moving from selling only coffee beans, you do not get the brew; without giving up enzymes, you do not achieve world-class drugs.'

Dr G. was visibly impressed. The presentation content and style was far superior to what even college students could have delivered. Prat Rao loved the way it had all started off but she was also a tad nervous about whether the next few groups would do as well. She led Dr G. to the next poster, where Aditi Chalisgaonkar and Anvitha Prashanth stood smartly, awaiting their turn. 'So what do we have here?' Dr G. asked them. 'Sir, we would like to present two entrepreneurs—one who is a household name and a resounding global success in the software services business and the other, a not so well-known name, who is a high-technology professional who returned to India and broke new ground against all odds to start a microbrewery.' Dr G. stiffened at the word 'microbrewery' but let the presenters continue.

'Sir, these two entrepreneurs symbolize two elemental aspects of great entrepreneurship: one is postponed gratification and the other is the circumvention of obstacles to find another way. The people we have in mind are N.R. Narayana Murthy and Narayan Manepally. Narayana Murthy, as we all know, founded Infosys. The company had a less than modest beginning with a capital of 10,000 rupees borrowed from Sudha

Murty and it took over twenty-five years for Infosys to come up as a global leader in reckoning with IBM and Accenture in the software services business. In its early years, the company struggled. At one point, we are told, it was on the verge of closure and the founders wanted to part ways. Narayana Murthy's contemporaries were leading comfortable lives as corporate employees, riding the wave of the information technology boom. For Narayana Murthy, however, success was far away. Then, a time came when he succeeded in creating not just hundreds of millionaires but Infosys was also listed as the only Indian company that created eight dollar-billionaires from its list of nine founders.

'Narayan Manepally, on the other hand, worked for many years with Intel in Portland, USA, and his one-time school friend Paul Chowdhury was in Motorola, in San Jose. The two had studied together at Bangalore's St Joseph's School and shared many childhood memories of growing up together as inquisitive and sometimes troublesome teens. After finishing high school, one had studied civil engineering and the other, mechanical, and had pursued different paths. After years of working abroad, the tug of the motherland endured and each returned to Bangalore on his own, not quite sure of what to do next. Then, one day they ran into each other at a high school reunion and one thing led to the other. Manepally had learnt microbrewing while in Portland, USA. He was fascinated with the process and was toying with the idea of introducing the concept to India. Together, the two started Geist, an enterprise that produced handcrafted beers. But getting the government to grant a licence proved to be a Herculean task because the existing brewery industry did not relish the thought of competition and made the going tough. So, after running from pillar to post, what did the duo do? They did not abandon their dream. While setting up a microbrewery was not allowed, the government permitted the import of microbrew. The two took a chance—they created the culture, took it to Belgium, brewed it there and, after paying a stiff import duty, brought it back to India to sell it at a high cost to discerning clients and started to gradually build brand awareness. What a strategy it was! Over the next few years, the government agencies in various states allowed microbreweries to commence operations. With Geist already an established brand, Manepally and Chowdhury took advantage of the new regime. They had a headstart over other brands. "Sir, to an entrepreneur, perseverance is key." Such an individual is not deterred by obstacles and a "no" simply means "not now". Thank you for listening!'

Dr G. did not like the beer part but loved the confidence and the charm and power of persuasion the two students exuded. He said 'hmmmm' with an appreciative nod and moved on.

Now, it was the turn of Pallavi Varma and Samvartika Bajpai. They bowed as Dr G. and Prat Rao moved to their poster. Dr G. smiled at them benevolently and taking that as a cue, the two started off like two birds newly trained to sing. 'Sir, we want to highlight the critical elements an entrepreneur must possess and then present to you two exemplars,' said Pallavi. Pallavi's dad had coached her on the secret of hooking someone's interest. 'Always publish the headline first,' he had said. Imagine having to trudge through the entire copy of a news article first to get to the headline. The idea of using the term 'exemplar' was Samvartika's idea. It was a new word she had learnt and she loved to use it everywhere. Looking intrigued and reasonably satisfied with the opening argument, Dr G. nodded to them to proceed.

'Sir, it is all about connecting the dots and seeing a pattern where others do not. It is also about the abiding concept of inclusion. Our first exemplar is Captain Gorur Gopinath, better known as Captain Gopinath, an army man turned organic farmer. Once, travelling in China with a group of farmers from Karnataka, he read about a young woman who had fled Vietnam at the height of the American occupation. She was adopted by French parents, and grew up to become a helicopter pilot. When the Vietnam War was over, she returned to her ravaged motherland and wept. What could she do to help? It dawned on her that Vietnam needed connectivity but had no road access. She decided, on the spot, that her contribution would be to start a helicopter business! Reading about her, Captain Gopinath realized, "My God, that is what my country needs too!" India's economic liberalization had begun, yet there were no solutions for a slew of critical needs such as aerial mapping, medical evacuation, and heli-tourism. Here was a dot but what about connecting it to another? That strand of the story lay in his association with his friend Sam, who had been an army helicopter pilot all his life. When Sam left the army, he had a tough time finding employment. Frustrated with the ordeal, he had accepted a job in a courier company. In fact, there were hundreds of pilots who had flown army helicopters and were now jobless. That was the other dot. When an entrepreneur is able to connect the dots, opportunities present themselves. They endlessly see the pattern of the future emerge! And that is how was born Captain Gopinath's idea of Deccan Aviation for chartered helicopters!

'Now let us present to you the next exemplar, Dr Devi Shetty of Narayana Hrudayalaya, the famous cardiac surgeon who had treated Mother Teresa and thousands of others. After having carved a great reputation for himself, he decided to start what he calls a "health city". The first unit was called Narayana Hrudayalaya. As you know, cardiac surgery is very expensive, anywhere in the world. In the US, an open-heart surgery can cost upwards of 1,00,000 dollars. How could the poor afford it? What about the rural folk? Dr Shetty learnt of the idea of riches at the base of the pyramid. His friend, the management guru C.K. Prahalad, had talked about it evangelically. He would say that the poor are individually poor but collectively rich. If you know how to sell to the poor, you will be a rich man. Dr Shetty teamed up with the Karnataka government and suggested the now famous scheme Yashaswini—every farmer paid up five rupees a month as insurance. When thousands of farmers paid that, it was a neat pile. With that money working like an insurance premium, surgical procedures for individuals in case of emergencies became free! Entrepreneurs who become high-performance and rise above the rest create unusual new value by including countless people in their circle of beneficiaries. That is how Skype, Google and Facebook today are among the most valued companies in the world.'

'Of course, of course,' muttered Dr G. and asked Prat Rao if she had a Facebook account yet. The two laughed and moved on. Aditya Roy and Pragya Gupta were ready with their well-researched content. 'Good afternoon, we want to present the two ideas we think make a critical differentiator for a great entrepreneur and makes an enterprise sustain over time. These are feelings. They may sound abstract but, we believe, entrepreneurial spirit stems not from the logical but from the magical, not from the rational but from the emotional mind.' They paused for effect. Dr G. looked suitably intrigued and pleased.

With a flourish, the two students continued their presentation. 'Take Ashoka founder, Bill Drayton, and MindTree's Subroto Bagchi. One is a not-for-profit and the other is a for-profit entrepreneur.

'Bill Drayton was a consultant with McKinsey. He was touched by the many social problems around us. Somehow, he felt that the best way to solve many of these was to engage the entrepreneurial spirit. He believed that entrepreneurs are people who see opportunities where others see problems. They are true innovators. So he created Ashoka. It spots social entrepreneurs and gives them initial funding and provides them the global network of Ashoka Fellows. Many among us may not know that people like Mohammad Yunus and Harish Hande were Ashoka Fellows.

'Now let us look at Subroto Bagchi and his nine other co-founders at MindTree. In 1998, they saw a pattern in the world's move from a manufacturing economy to an information economy, where every product or service would be either software-enhanced or software-constrained. They deeply believed that many Indian providers fell short of moving up the value chain and there was a window of opportunity to build a next-generation services company that would meet the emerging needs of the new world. That was about "feeling" a need. MindTree was not created on the basis of highly researched facts. The founders deeply felt there was an opportunity and they could do it! That is how MindTree went on to build solutions that make businesses and societies flourish. Take their Bluetooth technology. It goes into millions of hands-free devices that help us in myriad applications from connecting medical devices to driving safely. MindTree built the software for India's unique identity project known as Aadhar; Aadhar would provide proof of identity to every resident in the largest democracy of the world. Countless Indians today cannot open a bank account because they have no way to prove their identity. They cannot get a gas connection or a passport! Aadhar will help them in countless ways and make them part of the mainstream. While building great technology solutions, MindTree did not forget its social obligations. Its logo was created by a child with cerebral palsy and the company has been involved in supporting the cause of disability. Companies like MindTree prove the power of entrepreneurial initiative to deliver lasting value to the society. And it all begins with feelings.'

Dr G. liked the idea because it was a feeling and not reasoned thinking that had egged him on to start a school fifty years ago. He had then felt that Bangalore needed a merit driven, no-discrimination, no-donation school for the middle classes; now, over 10,000 students study in multiple schools started by him in India and overseas. He felt pleased with himself.

The next stop was the poster created by Ragini R. and Kartik Agarwal. They had decided to showcase two relatively unknown women entrepreneurs. One was Anita Shah, a homemaker who became the founder of a garden accessories company called Hybiscus, and the other was Lalana Zaveri, who, along with her husband Manish Gupta, started a chain of print-and-bind stores named Printo. 'We believe that great entrepreneurs operate in the intersection of love and competence,' they declared with feigned adult solemnity, 'and then the path presents itself.' Dr G. was floored. He could no longer hold his jaw up. His head was swirling and his heart was full. Prat Rao was gleaming.

'Sir, think of life as a graph,' said Ragini. Dr G. loved mathematics and the two knew this would be a killer line. 'On the Y axis, you have your platform. Every life is a platform consisting of education, experience, savings, family support and other such attributes. What we do with all that is driven by the X axis which is about purpose. Purpose determines how far we may go. So, the X and Y axes have a high and a low side and given the two, now we can mentally create a quadrant. Some people live low-platform, low-purpose lives. Some live high-platform, low-purpose lives. Some have high-purpose, low-platform lives and only a few can scale up to high-platform, high-purpose lives. We believe great entrepreneurs reach that. But at the start-up stage, companies like Hybiscus and Printo start off as high-purpose and low-platform because of their high ambition but small size. When they become successful, they move to the high–high quadrant.

Entrepreneurs start as high-purpose, low-platform but succeed when they are able to combine love for something and competence. Anita was a homemaker until she was almost forty. She loved gardening. One day, restless with her life, she went out to visit trade shows that showcased garden accessories and that started a quest. She travelled far and wide to understand the entire supply chain and returned to start her first garden accessory store, which became the fashion boutique of gardening in the Garden City of Bangalore. At Hybiscus, people can buy designer pots, urns, artefacts, fountains brought from all over the world. Today, she is successful and she is growing. She employs people not employable by the more glitzy IT industry and she pays taxes. She is successful because she built a business around something she loves.

'Lalana Zaveri liked printing and loved stationery. Her early training was with Xerox and she worked as a shop assistant in London, where she helped customers and sometimes even swept the floor. She loved the idea of retailing. So when she and her husband Manish returned to India, they raised money from private equity, something like an early-state investor you know, and started Printo. This is a chain of print-and-bind outlets run by high-school dropouts and people who couldn't speak in English before they were trained by Printo to handle sophisticated equipment and discerning customers. Operating at the intersection of love and competence, Printo is a great example of what makes entrepreneurs who they are.'

Dr G. was hugely impressed and looked proud. He called the group of students to his room and declared that he would like to present them with a trophy and a special certificate each during school assembly the next morning. A loud hurrah went up and there was much hugging and high-fiving.

CHAPTER 6

Suheil, Fly High and Polar the Bear

It was past ten-thirty tonight. The outside street noises were decreasing and people in the Daryanani household had retreated to their own favourite corners after dinner. Suheil decided to listen to some music to wind down. As he listened to Linkin Park dish out some nice rock, his mind became reflective.

Suheil Daryanani is a dreamer. He dreams to make it BIG some day. For now, of course, it is all about grades. He wants to become a chartered accountant but his real goal is to acquire some solid knowledge in the process so that he can start a business when he grows up. What business, he does not know. For now, that is not necessary.

This has been a rather hectic week for Suheil. He had tonnes of work to get done. He was also participating in a table tennis tournament at school. He had reached the semi-finals and the next week would decide the champion. He wanted to be the champion. It was very important to him because, among other things, he had not made it to the school football team and his arch rival Vicky Oberoi had! When the team was announced, Suheil was very upset but tried his best not to show it. His rivalry with Vicky was not confined to the football field alone. Vicky was a bit of an intellectual bully and always teased Suheil, irritating him with his new-found knowledge about the world of business, thanks to his dad who had a software company. He showed off by rattling terms like early-state investment, angels and VCs and IPOs. He knew Suheil's ambition was to be a businessman while his was to be lawyer, at least for now. As a lawyer-to-be, he donned an air of superiority. Suheil hated it. He hated the way Vicky treated him. The more he saw Vicky, the more resolute he became to prove that he could build a great business some day and then hire Vicky as his lawyer and keep him waiting outside the boardroom!

On that uplifting thought, Suheil switched off his computer and the room light, slid under the blanket, muttered a prayer for the impending table tennis championship and, before he knew it, was fast asleep.

* * *

In the beginning, it was weird. He couldn't quite understand why he was at a pizza parlour with an oversized golden hawk and a bear. The three of them were seated together. The waitress poured water into their glasses and went to get their orders. There were other people around but it was some kind of a blur—they were there and not there at the same time. Suheil instinctively knew that the hawk, sitting adjacent to him, was looking at him in a friendly manner. The bear sat across, solving a crossword. Suheil smiled at the hawk and said, 'Hi, I'm Suheil.' 'I know who you are,' said the hawk. Suheil was surprised. 'My name is Fly High. I'm an angel investor.' Preening his feathers, he added, 'This is Polar. He's a venture capitalist (VC).' Polar looked up from his puzzle, extended a paw and shook Suheil's hand.

Suheil had heard the terms angel investor and VC and private equity and so on—but he didn't quite know what they were all about. All he knew was that someday he had to know how to run a business and be able to hire Vicky as his lawyer. This was as good an opportunity as any to ask these folks.

The waitress brought their food and rather ceremoniously announced, 'Gentlemen, your orders!' Suheil wasn't sure he was a gentleman yet, and the two creatures with him certainly didn't conform to her salutation. The three of them took a slice of pizza each and started eating. Suheil asked, 'So how does all this stuff work? How does an angel differ from a VC? What do you folks really do?' Fly High spoke first. Polar had his mouth stuffed. And his paws full. He looked funny even though he put on a serious and somewhat official air. Fly High came across as cooler. 'Let me start and then Polar can add on.' Which was

good, because Polar clearly was the hungriest of all
the three!

***

Fly High started off, 'There was a time when, unless
you were born into a business family, the only way to
start a business was with your own money, your capital.
That prevented many people who had great ideas and
were willing to work hard but lacked the initial funds,
also called the seed money. Even though some people
started their own savings and borrowings from friends
and family, such enterprises stayed small. Very few went
on to become big eventually. Banks lend only to existing
businesses to meet short- or long-term cash requirements,
not to someone to actually start from scratch. In the
beginning, however good an idea or an entrepreneur may
be, they are untested commodities. Lending money to a
start-up in that sense has always been considered risky.
And for a reason—for every one that succeeds, dozens of
them actually fail and when they fail, they have no ability
to pay back. This is where angel investors come in.'

Angel investors are usually folks who once ran
their own businesses, made their money and are now
interested in putting portioned amounts of their wealth
to back a budding entrepreneur who has a potentially
great idea, not much else. The money is usually in lieu
of a small stake in the business. The angel investment,
as Suheil learnt, was to help an entrepreneur kick-start,
to rent the first office, to hire the initial set of people, to
create a proof-of-concept like a working prototype and
to get the first set of paying customers. Why are angels

called angels? Because, they come in without asking a lot of questions; because they do not demand this guarantee and that assurance. They have a reasonable understanding of the area in which the budding entrepreneur is going to work and can often help with contacts. But remember, they are not the ones that can give you a few million dollars. Depending on who you are talking to and how good your idea is, you could raise a couple of thousand dollars perhaps.

'Give me a real example,' Suheil said. 'Tell him the Google story,' said Polar, as he tried to extricate his lower body from under the table. Then he took out his Android phone and, with an air of importance, announced, 'Excuse me, I will be back after a conference call.'

Fly High took a sip of water and began. 'When they met for the first time at Stanford University, Sergey Brin was twenty-one and Larry Page was twenty-two. They became great friends and got deeply interested in the idea of computer search. Together, they built a search engine called BackRub. One day, their professor introduced them to Indian born Kavitark Ram Shriram, better known as Ram Shriram. The latter had earned a lot of money in companies like Netscape and Amazon where he had worked in his earlier years. Then he became an angel investor in technology companies. When Sergey and Larry explained their idea, Ram Shriram understood only so much. Yet, impressed with their passion, encouraged by the professor's recommendation and egged on by an intuitive feel of what might work, he wrote them a cheque for 5,00,000 dollars. Can you imagine that the duo did not even have a bank account to deposit the cheque? The rest is history.'

When Google was incorporated, Ram Shriram became a member of its board of directors and, a decade later, still is. Along the way, Google went public, its stock was listed and Ram Shriram became one of the world's richest people. Angel investors, also called early-state investors, come in at the 'ground floor' stage, as financial folks like to say. 'They are the talent scouts with a keen eye for people with great ideas and the capacity to make those ideas come alive through hard work,' said Fly High sagely. Suheil was beginning to like the bird.

Armed with money from Ram Shriram and another angel investor Andy Bechtolsheim, a founder of Sun Microsystems, Sergey and Larry opened their first office, hired their first few employees and started in right earnest. When a company like Google begins to gain momentum, it needs to invest in improving the product, by making it more robust and feature-rich. It needs to open sales offices and invest in brand-building so that it can become mega-successful. At this stage, when it is time to scale up, a VC comes in.

Meanwhile, Polar had finished his conference call and joined them, just as Fly High finished the story of Ram Shriram and Google. Suheil turned to Polar and said, 'Now I know how angels work, but how does your work differ from theirs? Where do you get your money from?'

Polar was beginning to like the young man. He liked folks who asked serious questions. Clearing his throat and taking a long sip of water, he started to explain: 'Let me tell you of the concept of venture capital and how VCs work. They are the major catalysts behind companies like Apple, Intel, Hewlett-Packard and MindTree as well as recent enterprises like Makemytrip.

com, Flipkart and Myntra.' Suheil knew the three names very well. For their family holiday, they had purchased air tickets from Makemytrip.com and he always bought books from Flipkart. Vicky, the show-off, bought custom T-Shirts from Myntra. 'In emerging economies like India, companies like these are poised to play a much larger role in the years to come. We put money into companies in their early stages, after they have raised angel investment and shown some promise so that some of them can become really big companies.' Suheil listened with rapt attention as the bear explained many really interesting things about his world. To begin with, he told Suheil where VCs got their money from!

* * *

'Think of educational institutions like Stanford, Princeton or Harvard. They all have large amounts of money that have been donated to them as corpus funds. A corpus fund is deployed to earn money for the future needs of the institution. Some of the money is put into safe investments like banks and mutual funds that provide relatively lower rates of return but assure higher degrees of safety. Now imagine that you are in charge of the corpus fund of a university. You are given 100 dollars to invest and the institution would like to make it 200 dollars in six years because that is how much money would be needed to run the place after six years. By putting it in a fixed deposit for six years, at an 8 per cent rate of interest, it will be about 158 dollars at the end of the period. So, rather than put all the 100 dollars in a savings bank account, as the university's fund manager, you could put 80 dollars in predictable investments and 20 dollars in backing start-up companies with the hope that a few may become the next big thing like Google and Infosys and the return on that investment could be mind-boggling. So you give that money to a VC. Like the educational institution, even banks and wealthy individuals invest part of their money with venture capital funds that people like me run.'

Polar reached out for another slice of pizza and Fly High chipped in: 'Let us imagine that Polar raises 100 dollars from various sources. He now looks for companies brought up at an early stage by angels like Ram Shriram that may need more funding. Sometimes he picks them up by himself, without waiting for an angel, if he finds it interesting and then he creates a portfolio of investments. He spreads his 100 dollars across, say, ten companies. All these investee companies give him part-ownership by issuing shares depending on how well both parties negotiated the terms for the investment right up-front. After say, six or seven years, depending on the progress of the company and prevailing market conditions, six of the ten may not do well and may even have to close down. Polar loses money when such things happen. In three cases, the investment may give a rate of interest that is marginally higher than the savings bank, making it neither a good nor bad investment. But in the case of two or even just one, the story may turn out to be like a Google or an Infosys, and the return can be tremendous because now Polar can sell his part at a huge premium in the share market. When he has made his money, Polar distributes the profits among his original investors and keeps some for himself.'

Suheil finally had it all figured out. Folks like Polar understand all about the world of investment, they know about the intricacies of building businesses from the start-up stage, which is a very different ball game compared to running a well-heeled large corporation. Very importantly, they specialize in particular sectors because each one has its own complexities and nuances. For example, some VCs specialize in biotechnology; some in real estate; some in retail and so on. That enables them to provide good advice to young entrepreneurs who have a lot of enthusiasm but may need help with the real world of business. While an angel like Fly High may write a cheque for an unborn entity without much clarity, Polar looks for a lot more refinement in the business idea because, remember, for Ram Shriram it was his money but Polar is accountable to institutional investors who have contributed to the venture fund. Also, unlike what Ram Shriram did at Google, a venture fund may invest much larger sums. So, when folks turn to Polar, he asks them to write down a detailed business plan. It contains information on the proposed business idea, an understanding of the market, ideas on how the company will make an impact despite competition, a forecast of its sales, production and other costs, profits, risks and plans for derisking.

* * *

Next day in school, over lunch, Suheil narrated his weird dream to his friend Suprotik Das. Suprotik too was keenly interested in the world of business but was not as sure as Suheil about starting a company some day. He was sometimes drawn to the field of law and sometimes to the idea of doing an MBA. In fact, even the idea of doing an MBA was sometimes confusing, forget about starting a company. He was intrigued about how large companies worked, not how they started. His dad, who had done his MBA, worked with Siemens. He had specialized in human resource (HR) management and was always at hand to explain things. Father and son made a fantastic duo and conspired like siblings, often incurring the wrath of a significantly higher power: the Great Bengali Matriarch.

CHAPTER 7

Mother Goddess and the Enterprise

When Mr Das returned home after a really gruelling day at work, he did not quite anticipate the eerie silence hanging in the drawing room. Had it not been for the part-time help who stepped out just as he was coming in, he would have assumed that no one was home. Gently, he turned the knob and opened the main door, took off his shoes (as was the regulation of the house), placed his laptop bag on the console and switched on the main light. Only then did he realize that his wife was sitting on a chair, all by herself, aware of his arrival and everything thereafter . . .

Twenty years of conjugal life had taught Mr Das two things—one, to know when she was really mad;

two, not to persist about the reasonableness of the root cause. Any deviation could result in an instantaneous, infinite loop of displeasure. Mother Kali's ire it is called, something every Bengali man learnt to deeply respect!

'Ki hoyechhe? What happened?' He tried to sound sympathetic and concerned; he could scarcely conceal his nervousness about whatever was to follow.

There was silence. Just silence. Then Mrs Das abruptly turned away from him. He had a terrible sense of foreboding.

'Aare baba, hoyechheta ki, bolbe to? What has happened now?'

Now she exploded like Mount Vesuvius on a divine injunction from the heavens. It was *his* fault that their son Suprotik was just not studying. Not listening to her at all. Instead of focusing on his commerce work for class 11—and, incidentally, his friends were already working on the question papers of class 12, as so-and-so had told her—this boy was surfing the Net for salsa and hip-hop or fooling around with his guitar or doing something else, everything but listening to her.

'Bhalo kore diyechhi aaj. Tumi khhechho matha ta!' ('I've given him a real dressing down today. It is you who has spoilt him.') 'Gelo kothaye? Where is he?' asked Mr Das, trying his best to sound serious and disapproving. Mrs Das signalled towards the basement, saying, 'Podte bosechhe hoito.' ('I think he's studying in there.')

Mr Das walked down to part-enquire, part-counsel, part-admonish his son. He found Suprotik seated on a bean bag, playing at his Wii console. He knew that his dad had come in but took no notice. It was a protocol well rehearsed. Mr Das walked across to where his 5' 11" scion lay and slipped his tired body into a nearby bean bag. The men did not look at each other even as Mr Das extended his hand towards Suprotik in a silent ritual. The console changed hands and it was now Mr Das's turn to chase the bad guy of the videogame in the tunnel. Mr Das loved it. The excitement soon extinguished the fatigue of work and the recent encounter with Mother Kali receded into oblivion.

'Hey, Dad?'

'Yes, man?'

'Should I study law or do my MBA after my undergrad?'

The question was a far cry from the impending CBSE examination and Mr Das absent-mindedly admired his son's resilience. But on the video screen, in front of him, the bad guy had suddenly slipped out of vision and Mr Das momentarily panicked. 'An MBA is not a bad idea,' he said, recovering his video-gaming composure. He marvelled at the thickness of his only son's skin. Looking at the fellow, you could not say he had just survived his mother's ire.

'Yeah, I thought of MBA as well, but I need to specialize you know and I have no idea what really happens in a company, what really goes on in there . . . What should be my specialization, Dad? Production, inventory, sales, after-market, all that stuff . . .' The bad guy in the video game was now up against a wall and Mr Das had his zeta-gun trained on him with the satisfaction of James Bond but then the villain simply dissolved like salt in water, just melted away, leaving Mr Das flummoxed. And then there was nothing. The devil had done it again.

Mr Das involuntarily uttered a word that was banned in the household. 'Daaad!' Suprotik chastised him. 'Sorry, sorry,' Mr Das muttered and turned to his son. The console changed hands and, under the more effective command of Suprotik, the screen villain was finally hunted down!

***

Meanwhile, the Great Bengali Matriarch knew the father–son duo's track record of shirking tasks at hand for chasing pipe dreams that could be as long as a decade away. She had an eerie feeling that the two were up to no good and decided to investigate.

She opened the door only to see a dark underground. As her eyes got accustomed to it, her penetrating gaze fell over the infernal father–son duo. The video game was frozen on screen and father–son were fast asleep in their respective bean bags.

'Nikuchi koreche,' she hissed and with one quick sweep of her hand turned the lights on and simultaneously bellowed, 'Tomra ki bhebechho ta ki? Aaj tomader ekdin ki amarek din. Dujoneri khawa bondo aaj. Chuloye jaao baap–beta!' ('What are you two thinking? It is either you or me today. No food for the two of you. Go to hell, you father and son!')

The maternal ire subsided only after a truce was voluntarily arrived at that Suprotik would study a chapter each of every subject every day, under the expert, involved and accountable supervision of Mr Das. Mr Das would further ensure that within a stipulated time,

Suprotik would solve the last three years' examination papers. And also, during the period of probation, neither party would visit the basement.

* * *

Mr Das first talked to Suprotik about production. From him, Suprotik learnt that production is no longer what it used to be. Once upon a time, it conjured up the vision of a smoke-stack chimney in a factory, blackened weather-beaten faces of toiling blue-collar workers, sludge and slurry and raw material entering from one end and at the other end, finished products stacked up in neat rows.

Today, a production unit is like a symphony orchestra. Every musician plays his or her own instrument and collectively, something magical comes out, something larger than the sum of its parts. The key to this symphony is a production planning system that creates an advance plan of what must get produced, based on orders in hand and at times a forecast by salespeople on what might sell. The production controller breaks the plan down to how much raw material would be needed and in what sequence, places an indent on the procurement folks who are responsible for managing relationship with the many suppliers. The production controller does complex shop-floor planning using sophisticated computer models. Shop-floor planning is like composing music and allocating different notes to different musicians and arranging the hand-offs and the takeover so that no one is idling. The concept of no one idling is not so much about workers but about machines. The moment a production plan is in motion, the output of one machine creates the input for another.

Imagine the paint unit of a car manufacturer. It receives the car body on which, based on the pre-planned colour scheme, it must paint a red or a white or a yellow. If there is a glitch of any kind at the body building unit, the paint unit may stay idle. An automotive manufacturing plant has many such interdependencies, all the way from a rolling strip unit from which a car body is made using coiled steel, to an engine unit that mounts the engine to electrical wiring to the paint shop, to others that integrate seats supplied by a sister unit or a contract manufacturing plant, glass fittings and lamps and horns and batteries and a hundred other things sourced from many different suppliers, before the final, assembled product is tested and certified ready to go. When the paint unit idles, it has rippling implications that impacts many dependent activities and disrupts a much larger system. So harmony is critical and hence we need a well-thought-out production plan.

The idea of production is preceded by research and design. Each part of the car has been individually designed from an initial overall concept. Based on prior research, design creates and hands over a prototype to production. There can be many trials and errors at the design stage, but by the time things come to production, they have to be good enough for customer use and it is the job of manufacturing folks to then produce things in a low-cost manner with no defects. The production person's life revolves around concepts like production plans, work breakdown structure, just-in-time assembly, zero downtime for machinery, flexible manufacturing, preventive maintenance, workplace safety and so on.

The concept of modern manufacturing almost coincided with the advent of computers. Though ENIAC, the first computer, was developed in 1946, the accelerated growth in manufacturing and the four generations of computers overlapped with each other through the 1940s and 1980s. Today, no production unit can do without computer integrated manufacturing or CIM. Many manufacturing units are no longer human-intensive; assembly lines are run by robots programmed by human intelligence. Once the production requirements are fed into a CIM system, it can automatically raise indents for raw materials, prime the manufacturing assemblies and sub-assemblies, line up the exact sequence of production and, sometimes, produce the items of manufacture without any human intervention in what is called a 'lights out' production line. The term 'lights out' means a fully automated system that does not require any human intervention or supervision so you can literally run a production line without any lights on!

An automobile manufacturer like Maruti or Ford depends on hundreds of suppliers of sub-assemblies and makes a close-knit ecosystem so that each one works in tandem with the other and there is an extremely efficient, very sophisticated handover and takeover from design to just-in-time supplies. This close-knit, mutually dependent system has come to be known as a supply chain.

There was a time when people would think of setting up the production facility first and the supply chain next. But, in today's globalized world, people often determine their production facilities based on where the supply chain may be so that you get your raw material efficiently and lower transportation costs. That is how most electronic products are assembled in the Far East countries because most component manufacturers are located in the Pacific Rim. Proximity to suppliers is a very important consideration. That is why an automotive company like Toyota has hundreds of suppliers within hours from its plants.

At times, though, a production facility may be set up close to where the buyer is. It helps reach the product to its end-customer quicker and at a lower transportation cost. That is how carmaker Hyundai builds its cars for the Indian market in Chennai while Suzuki makes them in Gurgaon. Today, India and China are the largest markets for passenger cars. This means that if a car manufacturer is not a leader in these two markets, automatically its share of the global market falls. So, from Ford to Honda, everyone is shifting manufacturing to India and China.

Manufacturing was considered the most important part of an enterprise in the last century. Now, many companies do not bother about owning their own manufacturing facilities. The concept of third-party manufacturing has come to stay in many businesses. The Wrangler jeans you wear may have been manufactured in India or Bangladesh by a contract manufacturer. Similar is the case with most branded garments sold in the US or Europe, from Gap to Guess. Many branded personal computers are manufactured by Acer of Taiwan and then sold under the labels of their respective companies. To an increasing number of companies, manufacturing is no longer what they want to 'own' by themselves—it can be 'outsourced'.

Rather, they own the research, the design, the brand and the distribution system through which the product or service is delivered to buyers like you and I. The people who manufacture something on behalf of others are known as 'contract manufacturers' and you hear the term 'outsourcing' often in relation to what they do. Look at the back of your iPod or iPad and you will only see 'designed in California'. Apple, like most electronics goods manufacturers, 'outsources' its manufacturing to companies in China.

Manufacturing has become highly sophisticated in terms of usage of computers and application of mathematical principles. Connected to manufacturing is the concept of inventory, to which every business pays a lot of attention. Both excess and inadequate inventory of items is a great cause of concern. It is a non-trivial issue for most CEOs and to get a sense of what it is all about, let us now turn to your mother's kitchen.

Over the next few weeks, Suprotik and Mr Das spent quite a bit of time together. When Mrs Das was out of earshot, Mr Das did patiently explain to his son all about how companies conducted their business. Suprotik was very fond of his dad and liked the way he explained things. In exchange, he taught him the ways of the Wii whenever Mrs Das was away.

***

When Mr Das started to spend time with Suprotik, explaining the many things that go into the making of an enterprise, a rather interesting thing started to happen. While the future-gazing and telescoping had no bearing on his immediate deliverables and continued to arouse suspicion in Mrs Das, the young man magically started putting more effort into his real school work, became visibly focused and even asked for money to buy question banks. Mrs Das was pleased but would not lower the alert level. But father–son knew that the charm was beginning to work. After the great conversation on inventory management—Mrs Das had eavesdropped on the mother's kitchen part—Mr Das lay on the bed reading a book while Mrs Das did sudoku. Sensing this as the opportune moment, Suprotik inserted his almost six-foot frame between the two and put his heavy arm and leg on his mother and hugged her. He was growing up like a beast these days and his affection was sometimes, well, heavy!

'Anek hoyechhe, thak esab ebar. Ja podte bos,' she said, feigning annoyance. ('Enough. Stop all this and go study.') 'Ektu aador korbe to?' He snuggled closer. ('Give us a little love.') 'Ei baap–beta ke niye athishtho hoye gelam ami. Ebar ja!' ('You father and son are driving me up the wall. Go now!') With that, she hugged him and got off the bed to make dinner. 'Hey Dad, that was cool, the production stuff. It makes so much sense now.' Mr Das was pleased with the acknowledgement. 'Yeah,' he said. 'When will you tell me the rest of the stuff, Dad? Like inventory and sales, selling and all?'

'Let's do that on Saturday afternoon after your mathematics extra class.'

'Deal?'

'Deal.'

The next time you walk into your mother's kitchen, look at all the items of grocery she has in her store. Count the number of things in the racks and the cabinets and the larder. At any given time, she carries an inventory of hundreds of items including perishables and non-perishables, utensils, implements, machines, cooking vessels, serving dishes and cleaning accessories. Her larder resembles a miniature supermarket, stocked with at least fifty different items from rice to spice, oil to matchbox. Look also at the things in her refrigerator, the items in her jars and bags and tins and cartons—the inventory for the production of food for the family. She has an expert eye on what is being consumed in the household, what is lagging the acceptable inventory level and needs replenishment and, periodically, what must be discarded.

She knows her family's consumption patterns. Biscuits and chocolates and juices and bread are fast-moving items; cake mixes and baking powder get used occasionally and are slower-moving items. She maintains a different level of inventory for both. Years of experience have also told her how much money to 'lock-in' her inventory, how much is neither too much nor too less. What items she must have delivered fresh and what she can keep away in the cold chamber for weeks.

An inventory controller in a large company does similar work. He is an expert who must, like your mother, know the consumption pattern. But because large amounts of money are now involved, efficiency becomes paramount. So, he uses sophisticated computer generated reports like an ABC analysis, which lists the amount of raw material in stock in terms of categories of items based on their cost of holding. The ABC analysis is his bible; he keeps a hawk's eye on it so that he has the right item in the right quantity at the right time. Even a slight mismatch could lead to overstocking (money blocked mindlessly) or the inability to produce when you have a customer order (unhappy customer who may not return). The ABC analysis shows items of inventory in terms of their values.

Whether it is your mother's kitchen or a steel plant, you will always find that an inventory consists of high-, medium- and low-value items. Statistically speaking, only 20 per cent of all items account for 80 per cent of the total cost of inventory. These 20 per cent are what we call 'A' class items and you want to focus great attention on their movement. Usually, 'B' class items are no more than 30 per cent in terms of numbers but account for 15 per cent of the total cost of inventory, and finally there are the 'C' class items that constitute 50 per cent of all items but together may cost no more than 5 per cent of the entire value.

In a manufacturing plant, in addition to the raw material for production, there are spares and other consumables. Consider a textile manufacturing unit. It must have spindles and bobbins and grease and furnace oil in the right quantities and they do not strike one as inventory items as much as cotton and dyes and other direct raw material do. Yet, without them, you cannot produce a yard of cloth!

Where the production man's job gets over, the task of sales and distribution begins. The job of the sales organization is to know where the demand is and fulfil that demand through a distribution channel. Also, where demand may not exist, the sales organization helps to create the demand using the ingenuity of the marketing arm. While the sales folks do the actual selling, the marketing guys create the brand-pull and help generate demand.

***

Selling as a profession is probably as old as the agrarian times and pre-existed the ideas of modern-day management. The act of buying and selling was there even before we had currency, when people only bartered. Today, the concept of the proverbial salesman spans an entire range from someone who sells a Boeing aircraft to someone who is a door-to-door salesman, though the latter is becoming a rarity in the big city because everyone goes to a mall or a dealership to buy everything from a car to a safety pin. The retail explosion through Walmart in the US, the Metro in Europe or Total in India is taking away the job of the door-to-door salesman.

Less expensive purchases like a book to in-between stuff like an airline ticket can be made online. But you would seldom buy an expensive computer, a car or a home without talking to someone and often, only after choosing the salesman first, do you actually choose the exact product. In these transactions, all of us are looking for not just a human being who would sell something to us but a 'trusted adviser' who explains the pros and the cons, helps us mix and match things based on our unique needs and sometimes, in the process, builds a lifetime relationship with the buyer. That is how you and I are more likely to go back to the same person when we need an upgrade or a replacement for something valuable.

The process of selling is not always one-to-one between the customer and the salesperson. In large companies that manufacture consumer products, from Ikea to Unilever, products are sold through their distributors who, in turn, sell to the retail store where consumers go to shop. In such cases, the sales organization is designed to sell, not to the end-customer but to the members of the distribution channel.

After the Internet became massively popular and electronic commerce became common, two new phrases have come to life—B2B and B2C. In B2B, a company sells its products or services to another company. We do not always realize how large companies are themselves consumers of everyday things! Just imagine MindTree with 11,000 people. On an average, we consume four cups of coffee/tea per day per head, not taking into account what we serve to our guests. That adds up to 44,000 cups per day! So, MindTree places bulk orders with Café Coffee Day. They raise invoices electronically at the end of the month and MindTree credits the amount to Café Coffee Day's bank account. This process of order to payment happens in a paperless manner. That is the essence of electronic commerce that eliminates delays and takes away unnecessary human intervention.

In B2C, on the other hand, the selling is between a business and a customer like you who may choose to buy your next set of books from Amazon.com. When you and I buy things from portals like Flipkart, the cost of selling reduces drastically because no human is involved and the cost of building the portal is amortized over millions of buyers. The downside is that you lose the human touch of the friendly neighbourhood storekeeper who smiles at you, chats about the weather and makes the experience very personal.

* * *

High-value items like a car or a washing machine have wear and tear over time. This is where we need after-sales service during the product's lifespan; we need accessories, spare parts and repair, apart from periodic servicing or preventive maintenance as it is called. To keep customers happy with the purchase is both a business obligation for the seller and, at the same time, a huge business potential. It is said that car manufacturers make more profits from after-sales service and sale of spares than from actual car sales. It is called the 'after-market'. So, setting up an effective after-sales service network and managing it well for great customer service and profitability is a matter of serious attention for every organization. The better its after-sales service, the higher is the company's overall reputation. After-sales service is not just for products.

In many cases, when we buy a high-value service and not a product, we may still need after-sales service. Imagine your parents doing phone-banking. Or buying travel insurance before you go off on a holiday. In each of these cases, there is a toll-free number and at the other end is a human who listens to your needs and helps you out with your queries. This is called a support centre and, quite often, it is not a part of the company itself whose products or services you have bought. In all likelihood, it is a call centre appointed by the original seller and is located in a lower-cost country like India or The Philippines. These countries are able to provide support services at lower costs because their wages and other costs are relatively lower compared to developed countries. A lot of after-sales service related work is getting done out of Asian countries now and this constitutes part of the business process outsourcing (BPO) industry.

* * *

In every business, two vital functions bind everything from R&D, production, sales and marketing to after-sales service. These are Finance and Human Resource (HR) Management, each highly specialized in its own way. Finance is all about money and HR is all about people. Businesses must ensure that they utilize their money wisely, monitor it well and make profits, part of which can be reinvested in expanding the business and part distributed among shareholders as dividends. This is the focus of the finance and accounting function led by the chief financial officer (CFO) of a company. While the finance part focuses on more strategic, long-term aspects like raising money, making investments, monitoring the global financial market and so on, the accounting function is all about keeping track of expenses and income on a day-to-day basis. Apart from raising money from investors and lenders, the finance function helps with the creation of the annual budget. This is based on a projection of all the expenses and likely income for the year. This in turn gets converted into a quarterly and monthly plan. Close monitoring of the plan versus actual spending as well as keeping track of business income is critical, and the CFO is the right-hand man of the chief executive. Because, if a business does not make money, it is really no business!

The CFO creates and monitors a set of vital signs with the help of a dashboard that must, at a glance, show the vital elements like what is the revenue against the plan, how much is owed to whom, what is the projected cash inflow and how much is the current profit or loss. The dashboard is literally like the one in your parents' car that must show all parameters of the car's health from temperature to fuel in real time. Large organizations that operate in multiple countries have sophisticated financial reports generated by a computerized system that show which product and geography is making money, where losses are taking place, where money is stuck in excess inventory or a buyer not paying on time, and how investments are tracking against the original plans.

The most critical instruments the finance function uses are the cash flow statement and the balance sheet. One tells where money is coming from and where it is being spent, and the balance sheet periodically matches the income with the expenses; between the two, you can tell how well the company is doing at any point in time. The finance function also uses a whole host of ratios that can indicate how well a company is doing compared to its competitors. By looking at ratios, one can build a 'scorecard' for the enterprise and businesses must maintain healthy ratios between investment and profits, shareholder's money versus borrowings from banks, and a host of other indicators to make sure that the company is financially well run. Finally, the finance function is the overall custodian for what we call 'corporate governance'; it ensures that the company is running in accordance with the rules of law in the country of its origin as well as wherever its products and services reach.

* * *

Over the next few days, Mr Das explained to his son all about other functions like quality control, knowledge management, information systems and administration that provide the backbone for the business. While the role of quality control is to enable each function to employ quality techniques for improvement, knowledge management helps the organization generate, package, distribute and consume knowledge. The information systems folks provide hardware and software infrastructure for everyone, from the production manager to the salespeople in the field. The administration looks after physical security, upkeep of all offices and factories and provides people with a comfortable workplace so that they can be productive.

Even as he was listening to his father, Suprotik's fingers were busy around a Rubik's cube. He could do both listening and solving the cube at the same time and Mr Das, unlike his wife, had learnt it about their son. Almost close to aligning all the sides, Suprotik looked at his dad one quick time. 'Hey Dad, what about the HR stuff?' he asked. 'Next week sometime,' Mr Das replied. Suprotik got up to go; suddenly remembering something, Mr Das said, 'Hey man, by the way, this Saturday, I am taking a class at IIM, Bangalore, for their Executive Education programme. Want to come along?'

Suprotik turned around, excited. 'Dad, wasn't that where *3 Idiots* was shot?' Mr Das ignored what he thought was a pedestrian way of responding to his magnanimity. 'It is a great place of learning, one of the top B-Schools and the campus is beautiful!' he said to elevate the conversation. 'Yeah, yeah, I will come along,' Suprotik said. 'While I teach for a couple of hours, you can just walk around and explore,' Mr Das replied.

On Saturday morning, Suprotik got ready on time, sat next to his father in his newly acquired Ford Figo and the duo set out. It being the weekend, the road to the IIM campus was less crowded than usual. On the way, Mr Das explained the importance of continued education in the world of business because the global market is becoming super competitive and more than money, machinery and men—the old-world 3 Ms of enterprise—today it is all about knowledge. Knowledge is not static. So, neither for an entrepreneur, nor for the professional manager, the classroom goes away.

Suprotik was not really listening. He was all too excited about the visit and his mind was thinking about what he would be reporting to his buddies even before the visit had taken place. The car stopped briefly at the gate, the verdant green campus suddenly presented itself and Suprotik was drawn into a different world. His dad drove up to the car park and afterwards they proceeded to the main foyer. 'I will see you here after two hours and then take you to lunch, okay?' he said. 'Okay,' Suprotik replied and as he was absorbing the rough-cut, granite-clad beautiful building with high pergolas and alluring corridors, the green cover everwhere, a rather non-businessy kind of man, wearing a Nehru jacket over a white, collarless shirt and cotton trousers walked up to him. 'Looking for someone?' he asked in a very normal accent. Suprotik did not know what to make of the man. He told him that his dad was taking a class and that he was here for the first time and wanted to just look around. The man told him that he worked at IIM and was more than happy to show him around. 'Come, let me show you our institute,' he said and Suprotik followed him. It didn't hurt to get a guided tour, he thought to himself. The man was very friendly, answered all his questions along the way and showed him around. During the walking tour, the two came to where Suprotik's dad was teaching and they conspiratorially eavesdropped. It was a long discourse on HR.

'An enterprise is not something that is made only of money, machines and material. It is, above all else, about people. This is where we have the HR function that is responsible for hiring the right people, training them, creating suitable reward and recognition systems, ascertaining competitive pay structures and putting in place a performance management system that helps people to do their best. In fact, within the HR function's umbrella, each of these elements have become so complex and specialized that there are specialists in most companies who deal with each of these.

'A critical part of HR management is the area of organizational behaviour. It has gained great importance in the last few decades. It studies various aspects of human behaviour in the context of an organization and deals with issues like motivation, group dynamics, and characteristics of leadership, the idea of conflict and management of interpersonal issues. As businesses become global, another interesting aspect is getting added to this list, that of cross-cultural issues. For example, Cisco has its main R&D in California but its second largest R&D set-up in India. The teams are not only apart from each other in terms of geographic distance but culture too. The organization has to help teams that are culturally different to work as one team so that they together meet the goal of coming out with winning products. Cisco pays great emphasis on building diverse teams to work together by making them understand each other's cultural nuances. Many organizations today literally "follow the sun" in the design and delivery of their products and services. Imagine a team working in Australia. As the sun sets there, they hand over the unfinished work to a team in India and, as the sun sets in India, a team in the US takes over such that the work continues moving round the clock.

'A good HR organization looks at the possible issues and conflicts that could arise from such an arrangement and helps people stay ahead of them. The HR team keeps an eye on the emotional well-being of the organization and uses many tools like employee satisfaction surveys to monitor areas of improvement so that people feel proud and productive in the workplace.'

After listening for a while, the two moved on. The man in the Nehru jacket took him across to the Entrepreneurship Cell, their incubation centre which had been set up as a place to hatch start-up companies. Then he showed him the Management Development Centre and from afar, the residences. 'Wasn't *3 Idiots* shot here?' Suprotik excitedly asked. 'Yes, yes. In fact, Aamir Khan and his crew lived on campus for many days,' the man answered. 'And is it true that Virus' house in the movie is in real life the Director's bungalow?' 'Yes, that's true,' the man laughed. After all that, they were now back to the main foyer and lo and behold, who was standing there looking at his watch? Mr Das had finished his class and was waiting for his son. Seeing the two approach, Mr Das' face lit up. He seemed to know the man with Suprotik. 'Hey Pankaj, good morning. What are you doing with my rat?' he shouted in surprise. Suprotik suddenly realized that he had not even asked the man who he was. 'Suprotik, do you know who you are with?' Mr Das was excited. Suprotik felt awkward, embarrassed. 'My dear son, meet Professor Pankaj Chandra, Director of IIM, Bangalore, in person,' Mr Das announced. Suprotik looked at the man in utter disbelief; he did not register that right this moment, Professor Pankaj Chandra had his arms around him in an affectionate hug.

CHAPTER 8

Sunday at the Sethumadhavans'

'You have no idea what she is up to these days,' said Dr Sethumadhavan, with a tone of finality, as her banker husband poured her a cup of coffee after their leisurely Friday dinner that predictably ended with a forward-looking conversation on the family's top preoccupation—Aathira Sethumadhavan, fifteen going on sixteen.

Mr Sethumadhavan was the regional head at HDFC Bank, and the one with longer hours. With banking becoming such a competitive industry and India opening up its economy to international banks that could get into retail banking, it wasn't easy to head the regional operations of a private bank. In contrast, Dr

Sethumadhavan was a general physician and ran her own practice. Like all mothers of teenagers, she worried to death about what Aathira can, may, should, must do and contrasted it with the dismal reality—what she was up to in real life! The conversation was triggered by an essay Aathira had written at her instructions with the intent to improve her composition skills because the young lady would not study English at all! The composition, when turned in, caused much consternation in the doctor's mind and hence this conversation over coffee. Mrs Sethumadhavan thrust the paper into her husband's hands and looked out of the window in despair.

The composition was titled 'My Interest in Life', and started out thus: 'I have a variety of interests. Mainly I love cooking. I also enjoy singing, debating and learning biology. I am strongly against any sort of discrimination, and I want to wipe it out of India. My dream is to become a chef and start my own chain of restaurants. If possible, I would also like to do research in neurology, and set up an NGO for women and children. I believe that you can excel in any field you choose, any field at all, as long as YOU put in your 100 per cent. I want to make an international brand. I want to create a large chain of restaurants and, at a later stage, set up NGOs and research centres . . .' Unlike her daughter, Dr Sethumadhavan knew at the age of thirteen that she would want to study medicine, because her dad and uncle had known it all along. She, nay, they, also knew which medical college was right for her. Less to exorcize Aathira of her 'variety of interests' and more to buy peace from his wife, Mr Sethumadhavan said, 'Okay, I will talk to her on Sunday.'

* * *

Father and daughter sat out in the balcony of their house on the sixth floor, overlooking the canopy of green with Sunday newspapers strewn all around. Breakfast over, it was the right moment, Mr Sethumadhavan decided, to have the father–daughter conversation on the theme of focus—its purpose, great urgency and the many benefits that finally pointed towards not just any IIT seat but the one in Chennai, not just any subject but computer science, not just leading to any job in the IT industry but to very-large-scale integration design and not just any assignment but the one in the land of milk and honey.

That brilliantly original trajectory had been taken by his sister's son from Mylapore and his wife's cousin's daughter from Navi Mumbai.

Aathira had instinctively realized that there was a ploy of some kind when her dad suggested they sit out and read the papers. She simply played along. It was written all over him but more than concern at what may come her way, amusement was writ large on Aathira's face. She so enjoyed parental naivety. She could even predict how he would start. 'Aathira, I want to talk to you about the importance of focus in life.'

'What's wrong if I have many focuses? What if I can do many things well at the same time?' 'That may be true but unless you focus and excel in any one thing, people will not know what you stand for. What you are really good at; extremely competent in!' 'Are we talking about something like building core competence, Dad?' Mr Sethumadhavan was startled. He was not sure if he had heard her right. He peered through his newly acquired reading glasses, with what he hoped was an air of authority. 'Core . . .' '. . . Competence,' Aathira completed the phrase. 'Like Intel makes chips, Fedex is in the logistics business and Coca-Cola makes beverages.'

Mr Sethumadhavan slowly removed his reading glasses, sat back, closed his eyes in fatherly delight and said, 'Tell me more.'

'Remember when you and I watched Rafael Nadal play Roger Federer, when we were in Goa last year? Did you know that, as a kid, Nadal played football and tennis and then chose tennis as his core competence? Then he totally focused on it. Even in tennis, he is not good at everything. He is really great at backhand shots and court coverage is his core competence. No one can do that better than him, and he is able to win because of it and there lies his competitive advantage. His core competence!'

'Focus, Aathu, focus. That is the key.' A fatherly attempt to regain control. Mr Sethumadhavan was delighted by the way she was clearing the way for him.

'But Dad, sometimes you don't want to focus even before you discover what may be your true competitive advantage. Rarely, people know it in the beginning; things evolve, like what happens in the world of enterprises.'

Mr Sethumadhavan did not say anything, careful not to disturb the flow as Aathira gurgled like a freshly discovered mountain stream high up somewhere. He waited for her to continue, wishing he didn't have to talk at all.

'Did you know that, in the beginning, it was customary for companies to do everything by themselves? If you were Ford, you manufactured the engine, the body, the wheels and the fuselage—every single component. Those were the days of vertical integration, Dad; if you made cornflakes, you grew the corn as well. That model became inherently uneconomical and, gradually, companies decided to focus, like Nadal, on one thing that they did best. For everything else, they went to the best and purchased components. This came to be known as horizontal integration. Companies shifted from doing everything themselves to buying the best. In the process, the component manufacturers could standardize and often aggregate demand from many sources and attain economies of scale. This helped drive prices down and create a win-win situation. This is the precursor of the theory of core competence, Dad, articulated by management gurus called C.K. Prahalad and Gary Hamel.'

Mr Sethumadhavan had read about the great teachers who had authored many books and articles on the subject and argued that without building core competence, no one could build a leadership position in any industry. Core competence provided unique competitive advantages, raised the entry barrier, led to creation of a family of products and services around the core competence and all that translated into higher end-customer satisfaction. Mr Sethumadhavan cleared his throat. 'Sometimes core competence is simply a know-how, a unique way of doing things or the ability to build a formidable business ecosystem. Like what Michael Dell did. Did you know what made him different and successful? It wasn't the hardware. Intel chips and Taiwanese motherboards were, after all, common to all personal computers. But it was the way the man managed his supply chain. That, and that alone, became his core competence.'

'I know, I know!'

'You know about supply chains?' Mr Sethumadhavan couldn't believe she did.

'Of course I do!'

'Wow! Tell me about that Aathu.'

'Not now.' She did not want to get sucked into the conversation that she had crafted as an escape route. 'I have to wash my hair,' she said, in a very grown-up way.

'Ah, that can wait . . .'

'No, Dad. I have to wash it before I go to the parlour with Mom. Let's talk on Wednesday, okay? But make sure you come home early!'

Without waiting for his answer, she jumped up from the cane sofa and was off. Mr Sethumadhavan did not like the thought of his little girl going to a beauty salon but that fatherly pain was swept away by the bounce in her step and the prospect of the Wednesday conversation.

CHAPTER 9

The Case of the Missing Homework

Frankly, Aathira had no clue what a supply chain was. After that day's rather spectacular success in neutralizing the matriarch who had waged a proxy war on her, she had all but forgotten about the unfinished agenda with her father. To her utter surprise, on Monday evening, just as she was going to sleep, he peeped in when his wife was out of earshot, and conspiratorially whispered, 'Don't forget! You promised . . . Wednesday!' For a moment, she panicked. Then, she told herself that there was time. And there was Akshay. Akshay Nelakruti. As soon as her dad was gone, she slipped out of bed, ran across the hall, picked up the cordless phone and called Akshay. Akshay's father picked up the phone at the other end and frowned. Why, he always wondered, did only girls call his son? Half of them would not even wish him, no pleasantries, no saying 'may I speak to Akshay?' They didn't even care to identify themselves. As if he was his son's phone attendant!

So when Aathira said, 'Good evening, Uncle,' his heart somewhat melted and he called Akshay. But then he hung around, partly to discourage a long conversation and partly to pick up anything that may suggest more than friendship. So when he heard his son say 'supply chain' followed by a longish 'hmmmm', he was quite unsure about what was going on.

After a rather brief chat, Akshay went back to his room, switched on the reading light and took out a half-finished novel he had hidden under the bed. After listlessly turning a few pages, he realized he was not following anything; instead his mind was fixated on two words—'supply chain'. It was a mathematical puzzle, as if, that was challenging him. Tomorrow morning, he told himself. For now, sleep. He turned off the light and was about to crash out, when the eyes of the family's golden retriever, Cyber, bore into him. Cyber always inspected him one last time before retiring to the sofa in the drawing room. But tonight, he seemed to have something else on his mind. 'Supply chain, did you say? Unbeknownst to the world, they actually spoke to each other when no one was around. When Akshay was only eight, Cyber was brought home as a puppy. Akshay read aloud his story books every night and Cyber listened with great interest. The parents had no idea that in the process, the two were gaining the power to transliterate human and dog-talk. It was a secret pact and the two liked to keep it that way.

'Yes dude. But you are a dog. What do *you* know about these things?' Akshay didn't like the intrusion. At times Cyber tried to patronize him, forgetting that it was Akshay who was older of the two. Suddenly he realized that Cyber was probably offended with what he had just said and was slowly, silently turning away. Akshay immediately relented. 'Okay, okay, I'm sorry. Tell me what you know.' 'Why should I? At times you all call me your best friend and then you call me a dog. Make up your mind kid!'

'You know I really didn't mean to offend you,' said Akshay, now seriously. Cyber was pacified, turned around, came closer and sat on his haunches. He was a big guy. From where he sat, he kind of looked down at Akshay who now lay flat on his pillow with the blanket pulled up to his chin, all the while looking at Cyber's intelligent eyes that always shone when he had important pieces of useful information. 'Listen to me,' said Cyber, 'the idea of supply chains originated in the world of manufacturing . . .'

* * *

Cyber was smart. He knew what would hook Akshay's interest. The kid was a car freak. Actually, so was he. Both spent hours watching Formula 1 and sometimes when the family went on long drives, Cyber longed to drive the family car. So, this once, he chose the automobile industry to present his discourse.

'There was a time, long ago, when the automobile industry took birth. With it started mass manufacturing at that time; the concept of vertical integration was prevalent. Every component and assembly that made up a car—wheel, axle, engine, body, hood, lamp, fender, you name it—was made by the same manufacturer. That is indeed called a vertically integrated manufacturing process. Over the years, the concept of vertical integration turned out to be inefficient for two strong reasons—specialization and scale. Imagine you are an auto company like Honda and your core competence is making engines. But now, you need to understand glass technology to make an impact-resistant windshield, plastic technology to make durable dashboards, semi-conductors to make chips that control the many functions of even an ordinary car on the road today, and so on. The list is mind-blowing when you think of a modern automobile as a whole consisting of thousands of parts and sub-parts. Each requires tremendous R&D investment to yield innovation and continuous improvement. Doing everything by yourself can make it commercially unviable because, after all, there is a cost to design and development.' Cyber paused for a while. Akshay knew he needed some water. Too lazy to get up and bring Cyber's bowl, Akshay simply opened his own water bottle and let Cyber have a drink. After two gulps, Cyber continued.

'There is another interesting angle and that is the idea of scale. Whenever you can produce something on a large scale, you can invariably drive cost down. The higher the volume, the lower the cost. So, if one company focuses only on wipers and researches the rubber and micro-motor technology that makes wipers do a good job, and then sells them, not to one but many manufacturers, the wiper manufacturer can have greater cost advantage. It can now negotiate better with suppliers (it buys rubber, metal, micro-motors and probably some more stuff a dog doesn't know) and get better payment terms as well because now it is a big customer for each supplier. This can help it to bring prices down and, in turn, sell the wiper sub-assembly cheaper to the auto manufacturer who can now pass on the cost advantage to the end-user like you and me.

'So, over the years, the auto industry shifted from vertical to horizontal integration. Every other industry followed suit. That is how Apple buys components from many suppliers and brings them to an assembler who puts them all together, puts the end-product in a carton and ships it to where Apple wants. Apple owns the design, the Apple brand, the quality standards suppliers must follow, the channel through which the products reach customers and so on. The same way McDonald's does not grow corn or make ketchup, though each is critical to serving every single burger. McDonald's focuses on developing long-term partnerships with its suppliers and influences better quality and lower cost practices with every member of the ecosystem, from the corn grower to the manufacturer of high-capacity pots and pans and cooking ranges. This is the essence of the supply chain. Companies must be innovative in locating good suppliers, train and guide them, involve them in the forecast process so each supplier has a view of the potential demand and then work in a synchronous manner to build an ecosystem.

'Thus, for many companies, building, nurturing, improving and at times even financing their supply chains becomes a very important competitive advantage. It can distribute the cost of R&D, lead to greater innovation and minimize waste by making and supplying only as much as a company needs. That is how Toyota gets car seats delivered by Araco in Japan, on an hourly basis! This is the origin of the term just-in-time or JIT. When Toyota opens manufacturing in a new location, it takes along its supply chain for a quick start on the ground.'

* * *

It was past 3 a.m. Akshay was listening intently to Cyber's long discourse on supply chains, careful not to interrupt his flow even for a second. When Cyber was done, he could hold himself no longer. Even though he was grateful for the discourse, he was a trifle irritated with Cyber's air of superiority. It was a sibling sort of thing. There has to be a story here somewhere, Akshay told himself and confronted the dog.

'Cyber, let's get to the bottom of this. Where did you learn all this stuff?'

'You really want to know? Okay, follow me . . .'

The two walked out into the courtyard where Cyber had a trap door. Through it, the two slipped out. The moon was shining and the neighbourhood was fast asleep. Cyber ran ahead and stopped near a heap of raked leaves. He quietly moved the dry leaves aside with his front paws and, from under the twigs and rotting leaves, emerged a chewed-up book. It was Mr Nelakruti's study material that had gone missing a week before his executive MBA examination. The cover read *Course Work on Supply Chain Management*.

CHAPTER 10

The Chemistry of Marketing

Priya Rao and Anish Kumar stepped out of the chemistry laboratory and realized that they had nothing to do until their pick-ups arrived 30 minutes later. It wasn't a bad idea to get a nice cold coffee from the Café Coffee Day outlet just a block away. As they were walking, Priya started what eventually turned out to be a long conversation.

'So, after school, what next for you?'

'Dunno.'

'No pressure from home?'

'Kind of, but not really,' Anish was distracted. A pebble lay in his way, asking to be kicked.

Priya rolled her eyes. Why must boys be always like this, she wondered. At Café Coffee Day, the two found that Megha Harish had reached ahead of them and was sitting by herself, engrossed in the pages of Amitav Ghosh's *Sea Of Poppies*. As they came to her table and dumped their bags with characteristic thuds, she looked up to smile her hello. Priya and Anish got cold coffees and joined her. Megha took a sip and went back to the book because she could not keep it down at a climactic point where Kalua, the outcaste bullock-cart owner, was running through a mob of villagers to save Diti, the upper-caste woman sitting atop her husband's dead body on the funeral pyre, waiting to be cremated with him.

Quite abruptly, Anish asked, 'Priya, what about you?' His strange question was directed at Priya all right but he was still looking at the coffee froth, as if it were a biological specimen of great scientific interest. 'What about what?' Priya was irritated now.

'What you asked me a few minutes back,' he replied. He was restarting the conversation that had paused a good ten minutes ago. What were her plans after school? That was what he was asking her! How strange boys were! He could simply hit delete on the elapsed time since the conversation reached a dead end and now he presumed she would simply pick up from there, as if nothing happened in between! Why, she wondered, did she have to suffer him in particular?

'I want to do an MBA, study marketing,' she said, in a rather grown-up voice. She said all that without looking at him.

'That's weird,' he replied.

'What's weird about it?' Priya was offended.

'Marketing is such a con. It is about selling things people do not need.' That was the longest sentence Anish had ever spoken to her. 'Excuse me,' it was Megha. 'Did you just say what I heard?' She shut her book in annoyance. 'Kinda,' Anish was non-committal. He liked her and she was a fun girl, sometimes pig-headed. 'Well, my dad was in advertising all his life and now manages a sports company and my Mom works for Titan, which is a first-rate marketing organization and, excuse me, I don't think they do con jobs,' thundered Megha, sounding like a New York district attorney arguing an open-and-shut case. 'If you care, come to my place and meet them before you say stuff like that, okay?'

'Okay,' he replied with feigned meekness and, without looking at either young lady, picked up his bag and walked out with a long-drawn 'byeeeee'.

'Jerk,' said Megha, pulling the straw to her lips.

'He is,' agreed Priya. Then, she said, in a somewhat resigned way, 'But kinda cute, no?'

'Excuse me,' said Megha, glaring. She couldn't believe her friend Priya had just said what she did for this creepy, weirdo guy. But then, that is how the three finally found themselves at the Holy Feet of Megha Harish's mom in her home office one Saturday afternoon, to be enlightened on marketing and branding and stuff like that.

* * *

When did the idea of marketing emerge? Its roots go back to the manufacturing economy of the late twentieth century when organizations migrated from creating a great product and then selling it, to actually figuring out what great products their customers wanted and then creating it. In a sense, it was the beginning of what we call 'customer-in' era as against the 'product-out' phase of the 1940s and 1950s. The latter had worked well in a monopolistic world where the customer had no choice. Henry Ford, founder of Ford Motor Company, had famously offered his customers 'any colour—so long as it's black'! Those were the days when customers were grateful for whatever they got.

Then came competition! It was no longer enough to make just any product and sell it; the emphasis shifted to understanding customer needs through sophisticated research and then making things that customers wanted. There are both quantitative and qualitative research tools that work in conjunction to unearth the unexplored psyche of customers. With that knowledge, companies create products that meet stated and unstated needs. That is the most important job of marketing. Marketing folks anticipate customer needs, create unusual products and service ideas, examine prototypes working with design and R&D teams, undertake pilot research for gauging acceptance and then build customer awareness and brand preference.

In marketing, the stated need of a customer is like the tip of an iceberg. Most needs lie below the surface. If you can penetrate and unearth them, you create innovative products and services. The idea is best illustrated when you look at Singapore's Changi Airport which is called an Aerotropolis. The word literally means 'airport city'.

How can an airport be called a city? A city is, after all, a large collection of people who live in it. But, beyond first numbers, a city is also a complete life support system in itself. You can live there, pursue many different interests and have a predictable support system like education, entertainment and healthcare. While planning for Changi, the designers had the completeness of a city in mind. They imagined that Changi would be like a city in every aspect, for the few hours of your life that you spend in it. You can take a shower, rest in a hotel room, visit a gym, browse the Internet, have Indian, Chinese or Continental food, lounge in a coffee shop, play a video game, go to a prayer room, take your children to a science museum or a butterfly park, buy high-end equipment, watch television, consult a doctor or shop for books or orchids or toys or real motorbikes without having to leave the airport lounges.

Talking about shopping, signs tell you to buy in a 'worry-free' manner. If unhappy with something you bought, they promise to refund the money within thirty days. They also pay you for the cost of sending the merchandise back. When Singapore's city fathers got feedback that Changi shopkeepers were not seen as customer-friendly, they mandated them to be trained in customer interaction skills. The thought process was to make Changi a desirable city in every sense of the word. That attention to detail made Changi a preferred hub for international travellers. And that's why all major airlines make sure that they fly through Changi. As a result, Changi makes money from providing berthing capacity, refuelling and engineering services to visiting airliners. Come to think of it, Changi is a well conceptualized facility and a well-delivered product. It is a marketing success.

Unlike Changi, many airports see their business as pulling people out of airlines seats and matching them with their respective baggage and sending them off. In reverse sequence, they separate departing passengers from their luggage and pack them into waiting airliners. This is called 'bum handling'. Doing it efficiently is critical, but that does not win you world-class status. You become world-class when you anticipate 'unstated needs'.

Changi's vision is to fulfil the unstated needs of passengers, apart from stated or rational needs. Unstated needs, on the other hand, are more likely to be emotional. When a company can go beyond the former to the latter, it can build a memorable relationship that makes customers come back, asking for more. Only in the last few decades have we begun to understand the realm of human emotions and the way they influence our behaviour at work, as customers, and factoring them into the goods or services we create. The real job of marketing is to deliver the equivalent of the Changi experience to every aspect of a customer's existence and create new value and customer delight.

* * *

The job of marketing is not just to unearth the unstated needs from a customer's hidden psyche but to work with researchers and product designers to create something that would appeal immensely to customers and delight them, making them return for more. This is called 'customer intimacy'. Acquiring new customers has its own cost. To any customer, a returning customer is always about higher profitability. After designing a product, the marketing expert must create a strategy to introduce it in an often overcrowded market. That is where 'segmentation and positioning' come in. Consider a pair of jeans. It is usually a pair of blue trousers made of durable canvas, right? It is just a commodity, one brand nothing significantly different from another. So you have existing dominant players like Levi Strauss or Gap or Wrangler. In comes NYDJ.

A pair of low-cut, hip-hugging jeans for a teen isn't good enough for the teen's mother and that is why you have a brand like NYDJ—Not Your Daughter's Jeans. This is what their website proudly proclaims: 'Some people say that youth is wasted on the young. But age has its distinct advantages. You're a little wiser, a lot more confident and face it—sexier than ever. You're not a teenager any more—you've been there and now you're past it, beyond it and happy to be exactly where and who you are. You wouldn't trade places with your daughter or trade clothes with her, either. That's not your style. Not Your Daughter's Jeans celebrates the beauty of women who know who they are and know that they don't need to impress anyone but themselves. Women like you. Slip on a pair of Not Your Daughter's Jeans and discover that comfort and style are not mutually exclusive. These are the jeans you wished for in the harsh light of the dressing room. The jeans you used to hope would magically appear in your closet. These are jeans that will respect you in the morning, look good coming and going and make you proud of every single curve—maybe for the first time ever. Here's to our lift/tuck technology that will make you look a full size smaller. Here's to defying gravity with denim. Here's to jeans that will never let you down. Here's to NYDJ.'

Segmentation is the art and the science of looking at the same pie but differently—not looking at a forty-eight-year-old working woman through the same lens as her eighteen-year-old daughter, just because the two wear jeans. Their ages, tastes, choices and spending power are very different. Now you can have jeans for the blue-collar workforce, jeans for young adults that are trendier or costlier and then you have NYDJ. Once you uncover a new segment of buyers, then comes the issue of positioning; the product or the service must be communicated in a way that depicts to the buyer exactly what it stands for. So, you don't get confused between Toyota and Honda. Toyota stands not for styling but affordable quality. Honda is positioned a step ahead where style, dependability and quality combine so that the buyer is willing to pay a premium.

A Volkswagen Beetle is a fun, young, cool car but in the same price range you have many sedans that are more regular cars, and the buyer of one would not go for the other. Every car brand and, within that, every model is uniquely positioned. Positioning is not limited to products we buy; it is as relevant to the service business, from hotels to bank, hospitals to consulting companies.

Trident Hotel is part of the Oberoi hotel chain but it is positioned to attract middle-management-level business travellers while the Oberoi properties are positioned to attract wealthy international travellers. Much the same way, Taj Exotica is positioned differently from

Taj Vivanta and the several lower-end Gateway Hotel properties from the same company.

Beyond segmentation and positioning are factors like advertising and communication, business development, building customer interactivity and retention, knowing each customer individually and mutually benefiting from loyalty by not just creating a one-off transaction but building intimacy and looking at the customer's total spend and aiming for a share of the wallet.

Just as Megha's mom finished explaining all that, her dad peeped in and announced that the children better go home now. It was getting late and their mothers had already called to check. The youngsters wished they could linger some more but they had to leave. Megha was, of course, very proud of her mother but did not show it, deciding instead to trade her admiration for something tangible on another day.

* * *

The week went by in a blur. It was Thursday. Priya had been really busy. That morning, as she was getting into the school bus, her cell phone buzzed. She fished it out of her pocket clumsily and looked at the screen. 'That was kool.' A text message. Nothing before and nothing after! Hmph. Priya deleted it. She was not going to be extra nice just because he had come along to Megha's house the other day. In fact, that day, they had hardly spoken barring 'hi' and 'bye'. Megha was right, he was a pseudo-intellectual jerk. But why was he suddenly messaging her now in his strange, cryptic, trademark style? She didn't care.

Soon, in the cacophony of the school bus, she forgot all about the text message. In school, she ran up a flight of stairs and turned towards her class, and there stood Anish Kumar. She ignored him and went past him at fast-forward speed.

'Hey! That was cool.'

She froze and then turned around. 'Whaat, what was cool?'

'Well, the talk with Megha's mom,' he said with a shrug. 'So?'

'Megha says we can meet her folks tomorrow evening and talk about branding. Wouldn't that be nice? What d'ya think?'

Long sentence. She gaped at him to suggest she didn't quite get it. 'So?'

I mean, 'I could pick you up from your place and we could go together . . .'

She wasn't sure he had said all that and kept staring at him. He had never visited her home before and did not know what to make of what he just said. He also looked a tad foolish just as boys inevitably do before doing foolish things. Before she could decode him fully, the assembly bell rang.

* * *

When the door opened, Priya's mom found Anish standing and by the look on his face, knew he was there to pick up Priya. She asked him in and shouted out his arrival so that Priya could come and be on her way.

'Priyaaa . . .'

'Coming . . .'

Priya came out of her room; she had been careful not to look dressed up. Anish said hi to her and the two stepped out. Anish had come by an autorickshaw and the two got in.

'Heard the Gym Class Heroes?' Anish asked.

'What's that?'

'The Band! Awesome!'

'Okay.' She wasn't sure what to do with that information.

'Adam Levine?' He looked at her.

'Ok! Lead singer of Maroon 5? I love them!'

'You got to hear this, okay?'

'Okay.'

He offered her an ear plug and put the other one in his. The lyrics were nice. It went somewhat like this:

'My heart's a stereo

It beats for you, so listen close

Hear my thoughts, in every note . . .'

The auto arrived at Megha's place just as the song got over.

* * *

The term 'brand' is commonly understood as a unique mark of a merchandise or entity. People think that building a brand means advertising. In reality, it is much more. The term originated as a distinctive mark on cattle that ranchers used when leaving their herd to graze, lest different herds got mixed up. While everyone 'branded' their cattle, one rancher called Maverick chose not to. That is the genesis of the term 'maverick'!

Emperors, too, brandished coats of arms. The idea of a flag is also about the brand of a nation. It is the logo or the visual identity of the brand. But, in the context of business, the idea of a brand is much deeper.

A brand is a perception in the mind of a customer. It is a perception of a certain value. So when I say Toyota, your mind conjures up images of quality. When I say BMW, you think of luxury. If I say Titan, your mind goes to another set of values that could range from quality, durability, affordability to the made-in-India tag.

The idea of value needs a conversation. Value to a customer is a combination of things, both rational and emotional. When a product or service satisfies our stated needs, we say it meets the rational criterion of brand value. When it goes beyond stated needs, it gets into the emotional realm and, together, builds a great brand perception.

A candlelit dinner, at a rational level, is about eating out. At an emotional level, it is about romance. A bike, at a rational level, is about going from point A to point B. At an emotional level, it is a young person's self-expression.

Building brand value takes sustained delivery of both rational and emotional benefits in a product or a service. Then a certain perception begins to form in a customer's mind over a period of time. When Samsung from Korea entered the consumer electronics business, people in developed countries thought it was a cheap, lower quality brand. Today, they don't. Perceptions can change over time. That is what brand management is all about.

We can look at a brand from another angle. It is about the 'intrinsic quality' associated with a product or a service. It could also stretch towards what is called 'aspirational quality'. The intrinsic quality is what values it evokes today and the latter is all about what position in the customer's mind the brand wants to gradually gain. Often, a certain brand denotes a business and not just a product. It may become synonymous with a set of rational and emotional values that lends its name to a range of products from the business entity. Take Nike, Adidas and Reebok—they were all shoes and then extended the names to adjacent products like sports goods and fashion accessories. This is called brand extension. Once upon a time, Titan meant watches. Now it also means jewellery (Tanishq) and eyewear (Titan Eye+) under the umbrella brand of 'Titan'. The marketing man must think of promoting the brand so that the products and services, which carry the brand, are received well. This is where advertising comes in. To reach the target audience, the marketing man hires an advertising agency that has creative people and media experts. These people advise him on the right medium—Internet, billboards, newspapers, sponsorship of a cricket team, whatever.

Today, every product or service faces stiff global competition. It is tough to rise above the din of competitive advertising. That is why advertisers now go a step ahead—they pay celebrities who attract attention and enhance the brand value through what they may be known for, rubbing off to the product, the perceptions they evoke via their own personas. That is why film and sport stars endorse soaps, watches, clothing lines and automobiles. When you see Aamir Khan endorsing Titan, it connotes youth as well as maturity, solidity as well as charisma and diverse possibilities like his versatile roles, excellence and standing up for the country.

Come to think of it, it isn't only Aamir Khan who has a brand of his own. Each one of us has a unique identity. That uniqueness builds a *favourable perception in someone else's mind*. It is a perception that stems partly from rational and partly from emotional considerations.

Megha, Anish and Priya simply loved the way Megha's mom made ideas come alive. When she was talking about the idea of a brand and how it meant value in someone else's mind, Priya could not help thinking of herself as a brand. And, why someone's dil went hmmmm for her and somehow she knew, right this moment, he was actually looking at her.

CHAPTER 11

Ghost in the Class

'Ma'am, you absolutely must do something about it right now!' Mrs Sharma, who taught physics, was livid. She had never been so angry before and would not go back to class unless Principal Chitra Rao agreed to take urgent and exemplary punitive action.

The offence was grievous! Jayatheerth S. was sleeping in her class. She knew he was doing it deliberately to disrespect her. How else could his subsequent act be explained, she asked Mrs Rao?

'All right, Mrs Sharma, but what *really* happened? What did he do to make you so angry?'

'First of all, he was sleeping. And when I woke him up, that boy had the audacity, Mrs Rao, *the audacity*,' she repeated for effect, 'to say something like Edward Deming and the entire class laughed!' She was about to sob.

Jayatheerth's dad worked for Synopsys as R&D director. He had inherited his dad's various interests, from classical music to reading an eclectic range of subjects. His professional ambition varied based on planetary movements but one thing remained constant— his admiration for Honda. To Jayatheerth, Honda was the ultimate company that stood for timeless quality. Its core competence was not automobiles but engines. Nobody made engines like Honda. It started as an engine manufacturer and continues to make engines for cars, bikes, outboard motors and light aircraft. The Honda quality is legendary. It has made millions of engines and legend has it that not even once has a Honda engine seized midway.

Often Jayatheerth and his dad took long walks in the neighbourhood park, talking about how companies like Honda made Japan synonymous with the concept of quality. That is how he received his first discourse on the concept of total quality management (TQM) and his father explained how the idea had spread from manufacturing to services to even personal quality. His dad had told him about the Six Sigma quality and how it meant as little as 3.4 defects in 1 million opportunities for error. Last night, Jayatheerth had stayed up until 2 a.m., browsing YouTube for videos on Six Sigma.

That is why when Mrs Sharma was explaining a particularly uninteresting experiment, she strangely began to transmogrify into Edward Deming. She looked like Deming and was telling him some really weird things about what happened long before he was born. After that he just went zonk and for how long, he does not know. When Mrs Sharma was shaking him, he was startled out of the strange experience and thought she was asking him Deming's full name. Thus he was now being produced for his alleged indiscipline, gross insubordination and wilful misconduct.

Chitra Rao knew that Jayatheerth was actually a good kid. Besides, having raised her own two daughters, she knew that teens can sometimes be very strange. But right now, she had to pacify Mrs Sharma and mete out appropriate punishment. 'You will stay back after class today and write a ten-page essay,' Mrs Rao delivered her stern judgement without looking up at either prosecutor or defendant. Mrs Sharma collected her belongings, thanked the vice-principal and walked out, only half-satisfied with the quantum of punishment. A few minutes passed before Mrs Rao looked up from the sheaf of papers and asked Jayatheerth what exact topic he would write the essay on. 'Quality, Ma'am, total quality management,' the boy replied meekly.

* * *

The history of mankind, as we all know, begins with the upright human who walked the earth some 4 million years ago. From then on, a lot of time elapsed before groups of hunter-gatherers settled down to farming. Radio carbon tests indicate that man took to organized agriculture at least 3,600 years ago. During this long history, it is not as if we did not do other things—we produced tools and implements, carpenters and ironsmiths came into business, people learnt to trade goods and services and sometimes they travelled halfway around the globe to buy and sell. But the idea of 'mass production' had to wait till after the industrial revolution in the early twentieth century, which marked the advent of mechanization and the arrival of the 'assembly line'.

The assembly line was a marked departure from the past in which workmen had to run all over the place to build something. In an automated factory, rows of workers stood behind the conveyor belt at their respective places and 'work' came to where they were. The piece on which a worker had to do a specific value-add, like putting in a wire or soldering it or fixing a nut, was programmed to come to the individual workstation, and then move to the next person as a 'work in progress'. The idea of the conveyor belt was conceived for the first time by Henry Ford, the man who started Ford Motor Company in 1903; this was the beginning of the term 'mass production'. Until then, everything was mostly custom-built in small quantities the world over. So in 1903 started a new phase in the history of mankind which, a century forward, led us to the era of global trade. But before we span that time, we must stay with the early challenges of mass production and understand how the concept of manufacturing quality evolved.

There is an interesting connection between quality and volume. Most of us can do a few things really well. If you play cricket or soccer reasonably well, sometime or the other you could hit a six or bowl a hat-trick. But if you were to do it season after season, you need not just strokes of luck but quality—you need to adopt principles of quality to your game.

Delivering products and services, time and again, with predictable quality calls for high-performance organizations. So, what comes in the way of predictable high performance when you have to play the game over and over again? Quality experts would liken it to the idea of variation. Given the need for repeat performance at your game, if you do not plan, do, check and act upon every stroke (PDCA), variations start to pop up in your game. In the 1940s, a group of researchers in Bell Labs, US, studied the process and arrived at the principles of what we all call 'statistical quality control'. The men behind subsequent advances in the world of manufacturing quality were W. Edward Deming and Joseph M. Juran. The former is revered as the father of TQM (total quality management).

To start with, people like Deming and Juran asked manufacturers to study variation by quantifying their work, setting 'upper and lower control limits' and trying to stay within the limits at a steady state to establish a predictable pattern of performance. Once the performance level was maintained, it was time to up the game and seek what is called 'continuous improvement'. Let us liken the concept to how you plan your studies after school. Say you don't like chemistry. You are most likely to avoid studying it altogether. But then, since sooner or later tests will be upon you, the night before the chemistry test, you will read the subject for hours. In this spiky mode, you are not in control. Your output and results are unpredictable.

Now you turn the table. You plan that every day, whether or not there is an impending test, you will study chemistry for at least 30 minutes. You place a chart on your table and mark the time spent on chemistry on the Y axis and days of the week on the X axis. You plot a chart showing how many minutes you studied the subject as a set of bar tables. Now, you are taking control and you have hit upon a critical aspect—you can 'manage' the process because you 'measure' it.

At the end of the week, your chemistry measurement shows that, more or less, you studied the subject within an upper control limit of 90 minutes on Sunday and a lower control limit of 10 minutes on Tuesday. Neither is good. It is spiky performance. What you need is sustained performance—about 40 minutes for three days in a row. This is the baseline.

Quality experts would say that now we should set the process at 60 minutes—the new baseline. So, the following week, you set yourself a new goal of studying chemistry for 60 minutes every evening. At the end of week two, you see yourself clocking an upper limit of 75 minutes and a lower limit of 30. But overall, you have set yourself to outperform your earlier quality standard. You are on a journey of continuous improvement, which is at the heart of every quality initiative. If you look at a manufacturing process, there is design, actual manufacturing, sales and service. Quality experts would tell you to focus on two critical things in this process. One, reduce defects in everything you do. Two, reduce the cycle time it takes to get things done. Defects are interesting. Every time there is a defect, it costs money to rectify it. That is a loss to the system. It is better to prevent a defect than to spend time and money fixing it. The aspect of cycle-time reduction is equally interesting. The lesser the time taken to complete a defect-free effort, the better it is. Because in business, time is money! If a business can reduce the time it takes to ship products and collect money, it can roll the money, that is, invest it in newer batches of production. Imagine a system that can produce and collect payment three times a year, versus one that does it only twice. The former is able to roll the same cash an additional turn and clock those profits.

Deming and Juran advocated the need for continuous improvements so that quality goes up while defects and costs go down, while continuously reducing cycle time in every activity. They evolved many statistical tools that could improve manufacturing quality in the American industry in the 1950s. However, most people did not take them seriously. The American industry was too successful—everything they made was bought out. It was a 'seller's market' where demand for goods was higher than supply. There was no incentive to become more efficient. Neither was there any competition.

It is very interesting that the country that embraced the idea of quality at the time happened to be war-ravaged Japan, which really had no industry. They were virtually rising from the ashes after World War II. They had to import food for survival and badly needed to manufacture things that they could sell to other countries and make money to buy food. Japan had no raw material of its own; it had to import raw material. The only way Japan could compete in the world of manufactured goods was by producing higher quality than the West but at a lower cost. They needed a smarter process, else they did not stand a chance. But when you lower the cost of what you produce and improve its quality at the same time, people simply love you. The island nation embraced the teachings of gurus like Deming and Juran and that is how Japan became a powerhouse, one company at a time. But how does one lower cost without sacrificing quality?

Deming asked the Japanese to systematically eliminate waste, something that large businesses really struggle against.

A business must track and reduce wastage of its own raw materials because they cost a lot. Let us imagine a simple business of selling lemonade to friends. You need several raw materials like sugar, lemon syrup, potable water, ice cubes, and so on. If you want to make it a regular business, see how wastage can start creeping in:

You buy sugar at 40 rupees a kg from a grocer but someone else is able to go to a supermarket next door and gets the same at 35 rupees a kg. You have wasted 5 rupees per kg of sugar.

You are too lazy to buy sugar every week and decide to buy for three months at a time instead. You overstock as a result. Some of the sugar melts in storage, some is eaten by ants. Now that is wastage.

A quarter of the ice cubes you buy every day melt because you do not have a thermos flask. Not having a thermos flask leads to wastage because you have to buy extra inventory of ice cubes.

Your buddy, who mixes the syrup, does not use a proper measure, relying on his gut feel and, sometimes, people find the drink too tangy or too sweet and return it. You make up for the defective drink and serve them again. You have lost money from your bottom line or your profits.

Your buddy did not show up yesterday and business was good; you had to get your untrained sister to help you and she broke two glasses because of careless handling; they must now be replaced. Bad production planning and poor skill training has led to avoidable losses through breakage of material.

You give the drink to some friends on credit and a couple of them do not pay back because you do not chase the 'outstanding amount'. That money has to be finally written off. Now that is wastage.

In management theory, whatever a customer does not pay for is a waste and must be eliminated. Imagine if the five wastages did not occur in your business, you could keep the cash with you and your profits would be higher. You could keep some; invest some in marketing your services via fliers in the neighbourhood and use part of it to pleasantly surprise your customers. So, Wednesdays could be 'bring a buddy and we will give a free drink with each drink you buy' scheme.

How much is the typical wastage in a manufacturing set-up? It can be as high as 15–20 per cent of sales of a company. People produce defective products that have to be made all over again. In the process, you consume electricity to run the machines again, not to talk about the labour cost for fixing the problem and the loss of machine time that could have been used for making other products—this entire avoidable process is called a 'rework' and the loss of money is termed 'cost of poor quality'. Thus, in a manufacturing set-up, there is always a great opportunity to look for waste in every process—from purchase to manufacturing to shipping to sales to service—and convert that waste to cash and apply the lemonade theory in which you keep part of the money saved as your profits, invest part of it to create new products and services and pass on part of it to your customers and build pleasant surprises that make them return to you. The Japanese manufacturers went after waste reduction in a big way and started making better products at lower cost and hence, more competitive international pricing. By the 1970s, Japan emerged as a global symbol of quality.

* * *

When Japanese businessmen learnt about the concepts of quality from Deming and Juran, they realized they had to enlist their entire workforce to realize the idea. At that time, the average Japanese worker was hardly educated because, till recently, Japan had been a country of rice growers. So, the concept of quality had to be explained to everyone using very simple principles. It is amazing how simplicity can catalyse quick grasp and adoption of ideas. Quality principles were explained to Japanese workers using fables and stories! Like that of the monk who was patiently removing twigs from a Japanese garden. A passer-by watched the monk at work for a long time and finally asked him how long he would keep at it. 'Till I am able to take out the last dry twig from the garden,' replied the monk without looking up.

There are interesting messages here. One, wherever there is a living garden, there is generation of waste. There are endless opportunities to remove them. Just when you think the last inefficient process has been fixed or the last element of waste has been removed, you see the next one. Thus, this fable inspired workers to keep taking defects or waste out of the system, as if they were dry twigs in the proverbial Japanese garden. In pursuing the idea of total quality management, the Japanese adopted a top-down and a bottom-up approach. From the top, the management made its objectives known to everyone; this was called 'policy deployment' and this ensured everyone understood what the larger goals were. The bottom-up part consisted of small, volunteer work groups that took responsibility to improve work. For this, everyone was trained on the 7 Quality Principles:

1. Quality is job #1
2. Customer-in, not product-out
3. Process, not result
4. Continuous improvement
5. Management by facts
6. Participation by all
7. Respect for humanity

These principles are amazingly simple and easy to implement, and not just in large organizations but also in everyone's day-to-day lives.

The first principle says that only quality goes out of the door. Nothing defective goes out. The only way such a principle could work is when every person in a chain of activity looks at the other one as a 'customer' and hands over only a defect-free sub-assembly so that the ultimate product to an end-customer is defect-free.

Imagine the process of making a car. The steel that goes into the body must be defect-free. The mould that takes in the steel and makes the body must be perfect. The engine that gets mounted on to the body frame must be defect-free. The seats, the glass, the door frames, the braking systems, the steering wheel, the battery . . . The list goes on and on. There are dozens of sub-assemblies and different people involved to make sure that the car that goes out of the door makes the final customer a happy person. This can happen only when each worker takes personal responsibility. Quality is not the job of an inspector at the end of the line. It is everyone's job. In fact, the gurus said it is everyone's most important job.

Next, customer-in, not product-out! During the early days of mass manufacturing, the buyer had to accept whatever the producer made because demand exceeded supply. Unlike in the time of Henry Ford, when you could choose any colour as long as it was black, in today's fiercely competitive market, customers can not only choose the colour but choose it online well before the car has been shipped so that the car is literally custom-made. The proponents of quality advocated that you could not simply push whatever you made to your customers; you had to work backward from what your customers wanted. In fact, a quality product is one that has been created with inputs from the customer. Every organization must incorporate the 'voice of the customer' into its overall plans and individual product design. There are many ways to listen to the voice of the customer. At times, it is through a formal satisfaction survey after a product has been purchased and used. At times, it is well before that, when a product is not even on the drawing board and an organization uses both qualitative and quantitative market research to develop a product that would make customers really happy.

The third principle is akin to the spiritual teaching in the Bhagavad Gita—do your best and leave the result to god. Quality gurus tell us that results are trailing indicators; the leading indicator is the effort. If we go back to the sports parlance, you train well, eat well, sleep well, plan well and, as a result, play well. Rather than daydream about the result, focus on the process. We only have control over the input, so that is where our energies must go.

To focus on the process is not a call for renunciation and detachment. It merely lays the path to the fourth principle—continuous improvement. Just like the work of the Japanese monk removing dry twigs may never get over, there is no limit to how much we can improve anything we do. Every process has three states—'as is', 'should be' and 'could be'. 'As is' denotes where I am today in terms of my present process capability. 'Should be' denotes my natural entitlement—this is where I should have been in the first place.

Our effort must be to move from 'as is' to 'should be'. Once we move there and stabilize, that state becomes the new baseline and we are poised for continuous improvement to the 'could be' level, which is aspirational. What happens when we get there? The journey begins all over again.

The fifth principle is management by facts. Human beings are driven often by perceptions and prejudices, not facts. At times, what appears true may not be true at all. Imagine how, for generations, people believed that the earth was stationary and the sun revolved around it, all because they saw the sun rise and set every day. Only when someone questioned the status quo did we really understand the fact that the earth went around the sun. The quality journey begins by asking for data. To manage by facts, quality proponents gather data, analyse it using techniques like the 80:20 principle and undertake root-cause analysis with the famous fishbone diagram created by Japanese expert Kaoru Ishikawa.

The sixth principle is participation by all. A quality journey is always a collective journey. A company does not become great in terms of quality if, only its leaders have understood the meaning of quality and are making continuous improvements. True quality improvement takes place when the entire organization is involved, from the lowest level worker to the CEO, and every individual feels equally empowered and responsible for it.

The last principle is respect for humanity. A business organization is not an island. It must give back to the world benefits like greater customer satisfaction and profits. Respect for humanity can also be inclusivity of concern for the planet. This is why Toyota started its green initiative in the early 1990s, even before the word green was in vogue. Sustainable business practices stem from the idea of respect for humanity, which is also about inclusion of external agencies to participate in and benefit from the quality journey of an organization.

By embracing the idea of total quality and extending it to every aspect of their existence, the Japanese transformed their country after their collapse in World War II and became an economic powerhouse. They showed their greatness by instituting the highest quality award in Japan in the name of Deming himself, who now lives on in the hearts and minds of the Japanese.

* * *

When Jayatheerth's father called his mother to deliver the news, she was in a conference with an important client. Knowing that this must be something out of the ordinary, she excused herself for a minute and spoke to him. There was a call from the school, she learnt, and Jayatheerth had been detained after school for some reason. It sounded rather strange. She knew well about all the homework he ever needed to turn in. And he wasn't the sort of kid who would get into unnecessary trouble with his fellow students. Somehow, she did not like the word 'detained'; it did not sound auspicious.

She told her husband she would finish her meeting and pick Jayatheerth from school at 7 p.m. She was wondering what her boy had been up to. As soon as she got free later that afternoon, she called Mrs Rao, whom she had known for some time now. To her surprise, Mrs Rao said that nothing was wrong and that she had just asked the boy to write an article on Japan's quest for quality for the school magazine, which is why he didn't board the bus today, and wasn't her boy rather good?

How did he learn all this stuff? 'By the way, do make sure,' she added, 'that he gets to sleep on time. Boys and girls need to put in so much work these days and the days are so long, they often get tired and don't realize what is going on. There's too much pressure from all you parents. It's important to not just fret over studies and friends. Food, rest and such things are so vital.'

CHAPTER 12

Facebook Face-off

When Samvartika Bajpai got the Facebook friend request from Rohit Pattanaik, she did not quite know the history of the social networking site. After Rohit invited her, quite coincidentally, she saw the movie *The Social Network*. Soon she became a Facebook convert and spent at least two hours a day on the site. On an average, she checked her profile five times a day for updates.

Samvartika and her Facebook friends quickly found out that in addition to being just a social networking place, the site could be a great place to collaborate on many things. After all, ideas build on ideas. When one person posted something interesting, others got notified, people came forward with their knowledge and opinion and soon there was a flood of useful information!

One day, she had a rather long conversation with her cousin who had come to India on a vacation. Her cousin worked for Intel and had filed three patents already. He told her that it was so difficult to achieve that in India for many reasons. Samvartika was very sad. She posted her thoughts on her Facebook page.

It was a passionate post about why the West had been way ahead of countries like India in filing more patents even as we produced more engineers every year. We were always in the catch-up mode. It had to do with a social system that forced us to produce clones, not original thinkers. Beyond the frontier of quality, what the nation needed was urgent reforms and that all of us need to think about innovation so that we could create products and services that did not merely copy the West.

'We have a raw material mindset in this country,' she lamented. 'We are happier exporting silk than owning designer labels. We export granite but don't make monuments. We are happy renting out our software engineers but don't attempt to make a Microsoft out of India. Why?'

Pragya was the first to 'like' her post but reminded her that India was also the country that had given the world the zero, invented chess and created architectural masterpieces in Harappa and Hampi at a time when the West was overrun by wild beasts. 'This is the country,' she reminded others, 'that created the Sun Temple and the Taj Mahal.'

'We don't live in the past lady, we live in the future.' That was a trite rejoinder by Pallavi. 'Indians are not innovative like the Americans, the Swiss, the Germans, or the Japanese.'

The conversation was getting interesting and started drawing many thumbs up and more joined in the fray and soon the entire gang got involved.

The issue wasn't social innovation as much as innovation in the world of business. Why can't we file original drug patents? Why is the Indian pharmaceutical industry happy with bulk drug exports, contract research and manufacturing? Are we a nation of risk-averse people? Why don't Indian businesses spend more money on R&D?

'The history of innovation tells you that it is not something that business can do in isolation. Companies do not innovate—people do. Where are the innovative Indians, duh? Where are the folk who pursue what they deeply believe in and come up with path-breaking ideas to create the next iPad or high-yielding, pest-resistant crop?' This was Nivrith. He got three thumbs up.

'I get the feeling that we are a defensive lot here. Didn't we make the Nano?' posted Vicky, the litigation lawyer in the making.

'Dude, what do *you* know? Gimme a break! Do you know how many Nanos caught fire going from the showroom to the customer?' It was his arch rival Suheil taking a potshot.

'I beg your pardon sir, do you know how many cars Toyota and Honda have recalled in the history of their existence? Would you care to note that Toyota vehicles started braking by themselves at high speeds and the company was clueless and there was worldwide controversy and vehicle recall? It is the middle-class mindset of Indians that does not like to deal with the ideas of risk and failure. We are a risk-averse nation. We create job-seekers, not job-makers. By your logic, Columbus should have been publicly hanged for getting his direction completely wrong, discovering the Americas while the charter was to find India.' Vicky shot back with all guns blazing.

'Wait a minute guys!' It was Rohit, always the voice of reason. 'Why don't we all get together and invite someone like Tanmay's dad one day to speak to us? He would know.'

Tanmay's dad was admired for his approachability and his interesting outlook on various issues. Though he was a top cop, most of his work related to information technology and management. All of them 'liked' the idea of getting him over and, after some quick consultations with their teachers, Mr Sanjay Sahay was duly approached and of course he was very kind to agree to address the students the following Friday, after school.

***

Word quickly went around that Mr Sahay was coming to school to talk on innovation. It was on every Facebook update, even some younger teachers tweeted secretly. On Friday evening, there was no standing room in the large auditorium. Mr Sahay was received ceremoniously by Dr Bindu Hari and took the podium to deliver a fantastic speech.

Tanmay was very worried that his dad would make a fool of himself and stayed out of the limelight, choosing to stand at the far end, watching from behind two taller boys. But his anxiety was misplaced. Within moments, even Tanmay was listening intently. His father explained ideas and concepts with simple illustrations and everyone super-liked it.

He started by explaining that the idea of innovation cannot be understood by just looking at one industry or the other. There is something ecological about it, he said. 'Why do trees grow strong and tall in the rainforests? It is because of the ecosystem. When a seed falls, the ground is fertile. Then there is a mutually dependent, complex system that encourages competition and growth and, in the process, the rainforest becomes the world's most beautiful collection of flora and fauna. Now, think of that seed I just spoke about as an idea and ask yourself, in which organization, which region or which country would an idea have the best chance? It depends on the ecosystem that the organization or the country has and it is very difficult to simply copy it. That is why Toyota is in Japan and HP and Facebook are in California and Infosys and MindTree are in Bangalore. What is the rainforest-like ecosystem equivalent here? It is the mutually dependent elements like good educational institutions, good living, and at times good weather, presence of an intelligent press, art, literature, culture and demographic diversity. Monochromatic societies, which are uni-language, uni-religion and insist on isolation, seldom innovate. So building diversity like a rainforest is very essential.'

Then he explained how innovation has linkage to risk-taking ability and isn't all about raising or losing money. The idea of risk, he explained, is very personal.

In India, we have a conformist social upbringing. We feel devastated if the child does not study engineering or medicine to get the highest paying job, ahead of cousins and neighbours. If the same kid is allowed to pursue his own ideas, because he now does what he loves doing, there are higher possibilities that he would innovate. But that is a matter of risk and unless we let him take the risk, nothing great would come about! We don't let the child experiment, fail some before succeeding by finding true love, as Steve Jobs would say. He illustrated how, in India, a failed entrepreneur would not get funding a second time but in the Silicon Valley, he is a hot commodity. A venture capitalist prefers a person who won't make the same mistakes with *his* money.

Then he said something very profound. 'All innovation begins with inclusion. When we take an inclusive view of things, the mind leaps forth with innovative ideas. Inclusion is about feelings for people who are sometimes twice, three times, many times removed from us. When we make a difference to them, it is usually through an act of innovation. You can always serve your immediate customer or supplier with linear improvements; something that is "new and improved", something that is "renovated" and not innovated. On the other hand, if you want to make a big difference to your customer's customer or your supplier's supplier—people twice removed—it calls for innovative thinking. You have to start with a zero base, as you would probably have to first understand their world. Now you may find that you are out of your depth in that world because you are in previously unchartered territory, the mind suspends all preconceived notions. You are open to new ideas. You experiment. And then the big things happen.' That is how Apple, the computer company, became the hottest phone company in the world!

After the lecture, Dr Bindu Hari opened the floor for questions. Vicky raised his hand first. How long, he asked, would Indians take to beat the Japanese in the automotive business? He wanted the 'Facebook Face-off' to continue.

Mr Sahay explained that the issue was not just about cars but about how a nation relates to the concept of knowledge itself, because innovation stems from knowledge. He quoted Prof. Yves Doz of INSEAD to explain that innovation stems from converting knowledge into something valuable. According to Doz, we relate to knowledge at three different levels. At the lowest level, we relate to it in a technical context where knowledge is all about specifications handed out to engineers. This can be called the adaptive layer.

Next is the experiential layer of knowledge. This is not about hand-me-down technical specifications and functionality, but about getting into the shoes of the end-user. Mr Sahay gave the example of how Nissan wanted to design a car for the European market. The company sent a delegation of auto designers who rented different makes of cars and drove around thousands of kilometres all over Europe to understand what it meant to be a motorist in Europe. They sought out the motoring experience on the French Alps, the Italian country side, the German Autobahn; all vastly different from each other. Then they came back and designed a car that was right for the European market.

Beyond the experiential level is the existential level, where knowledge is not about getting into the shoes but 'creeping into the minds' of end-users. When Sony designed the Walkman, it was operating at this level. Sony is Sony not because it manages 5,000 products or knows its Digital Signal Processing (DSP) chips and liquid crystal displays and ferrite magnets. What makes it Sony is that it understands what goes on inside the head of the kid in the Bronx when he plugs in his earphones. Sony works backwards from that experience to design innovative products and services. Sony gets it right at the existential level.

Everyone simply loved the illustration and understood that the challenge is to think at an existential level and not be a country of reverse engineers at everything, from music to fashion to services.

Another hand went up. It was Pallavi. She wanted to know why innovation is always seen as complexity; why we think of it as something way out of the ordinary. She made a passionate statement about how Mother Nature was the ultimate innovator. She said, 'The state of nature is about simplicity. The state of human thought has become progressively complex because we seek sophistication over simplicity. The most wonderful things in the world are also the simplest. Simplicity de-layers confusion. The world of art, literature and culture is a lot simpler than that of engineering. We over-celebrate engineering and the innovative spirit probably calls for a greater understanding of and encouragement for the liberal arts!'

'You are so on the ball,' replied Mr Sahay. 'Let me talk about my encounter with simplicity and innovation.

Recently, someone gifted me an iPod. My wife, who is not a gadget freak, loved it. I gave it to her. She visited her parents. Her father is seventy-two and her mother is sixty-five, retired folk both. When her mother held the little white gizmo and listened to it, the connection was instant. She did not feel challenged in any way. When she asked how much it cost, my wife gifted it to her. She accepted it only after my wife promised that she would buy one for herself. When I bought her one, my two children felt it was time they also got one each. What does the iPod give to the teenager? The teenager wants to store all things nice. She wants to hoard her favourite possessions from clothes to perfumes to music! And she wants to live in the clutter of her cupboard. But she wants to be able to get in and out of her favourite clothes whenever she wants, wherever she wants. If music is like clothes—which it is to teens—she wants to be able to carry her messy cupboard with her and look cool while doing it. The iPod gives her that capability in a suburban train, around the campus, at a party, in her bed, on the couch . . .' So simple and great! If you can figure out people's need and help them deal with it, sans complexity, that is innovation!

Yet another hand went up. Karan wanted to understand the linkage between innovation and adoption. Are some societies 'early adopters' and when there is a greater social urge to try new things, innovators are encouraged to churn out new ideas and convert them into products and services?

Mr Sahay was stumped by the question. He took a long sip of water and said, 'You are right. The greatest test of innovation is in its adoption—adoption by millions of people to whom a simple solution for an everyday problem makes a big difference. That is why the world loves Lycra; that is why every mother wants her teenager to carry a cell phone and is also willing to pay for it; that is why the digital camera has changed our way of thinking about photography. Any innovation that requires sophisticated understanding has elitism built into its social contract, and therefore has limited adoption. The world is hungry for things it can easily understand, touch, feel, smell, hold, carry and sometimes throw away like contact lenses and disposable razors.'

Mr Ramanathan, the commerce teacher, raised his hand. He made an impassioned statement that made people wonder what the question was. 'The last time we built something unique and gave it to the world was . . . when? After Hampi and the Taj, for hundreds of years, a nation has hibernated. We have not built anything architecturally unique. From Lutyen's Delhi to the Mysore Palace to the Bahai Temple in New Delhi to Howrah Bridge, each is only reminiscence. When a nation flounders in an architectural sense, it also flounders in every other aspect of creativity. Creative fields like art, literature, music, dance, fashion and architectural design are all interlinked with scientific quest, geographic exploration and spiritualism. By looking at the architectural design of a civilization at a given time, one can immediately understand what was going on in the minds of people who lived in it. Architecture externalizes everything else. When India stopped building temples, mosques, courtyards and stepped wells, India also slid from the existential layer to the adaptive. Do you see an escape?' Can the world of business break free from the shackles of a social past?

It wasn't a question; it was a speech, with its conclusion couched as a question. Being a seasoned bureaucrat, Mr Sahay effortlessly answered: 'I think all this is about to undergo a change. I believe that we are in the cusp of a millennial shift in which India will once again innovate. I see the first signs of spring after the civilizational hibernation that afflicted an entire people for the last few centuries. I see that unmistakable step of spring in the fiction of Vikram Seth and Jhumpa Lahiri and Arundhati Roy, who are telling the world that people with difficult-to-pronounce names can write for a global audience. I see the signs when people across the world curl up on their couches to scream or smile at the will of Manoj Night Shyamalan and Mira Nair and Gurinder Chadha. I see a nation of silkworm-breeders and cotton-weavers begin to drape the world's supermodels with the sensuousness of a Ritu Beri or Tarun Tahiliani. All this also extends to the spheres of sports and hospitality, healthcare and drug research. Yes, in saying all this, I risk crossing over from being the voice of reason to the voice of hope—but that is a risk I am willing to take. I believe India's time has come. India will innovate!'

The hall erupted with thunderous applause, the students and staff gave him a standing ovation. Meanwhile, danger was clearly raising its head someplace else in the form of another Facebook Face-off.

* * *

Unknown to Rohit Pattanaik, whose tryst with Facebook had got the innovation engine revving, his love for it had also catalysed unexpected events elsewhere. It all started with the middle-aged, slightly pot-bellied, part-time sports coach with a receding hairline who came to teach the 'boys and girls' a few elementary games and gymnastics but was soon found claiming that he could coach them in everything from decathlons to rowing to basketball to archery. His name was Chinnaswamy Nageshwara Rao, but he liked to introduce himself as Nags. There was mystery surrounding his origin and achievements; someone said he nearly qualified for the Olympics in some obscure sport, someone else said he never went beyond the Commonwealth Games, a few claimed that he was just a local body builder in his youth, nobody was quite sure of his core competence. Everyone humoured him because it could mean the difference between goofing off and running around the school field in the most mindless manner. Despite his unclassified existence, Nags could cause trouble.

Rohit was nice to everyone and very helpful. So when one day, Nags Sir asked him to create a Gmail account for him, Rohit was very happy to do so. He taught Nags Sir how to compose and send e-mails. It was a great achievement and Rohit felt deep satisfaction at bridging the digital divide, one man at a time. Soon, however, trouble started. Nags Sir got hundreds of chain mails every month and, without rhyme or reason, forethought or remorse, forwarded them to everyone in his mailbox. Rohit regretted the technological conversion he had undertaken. So, he decided to give Nags Sir a more eclectic diversion—Facebook.

What a change Facebook brought to Chinnaswamy Nageshwara Rao's existence. He first invited everyone in his mailbox to be his friend. He just loved the idea. Then came friends recommended by friends, some of whom he had never met. Somehow, that in itself made it an alluring experience, a communion like never before. His days were incomplete without friend requests and he loved accepting them, going to their walls and posting comments and loved how many of them returned the favour. Late one evening, as he was Facebooking, the doorbell rang. His neighbour Nanje Gowda had a rather urgent matter to discuss. As the two men stood outside conversing, Mrs Jagadamba Nageshwara Rao came looking for her husband and not finding him at his desk, peered at the computer screen instead, only to see his profile and frowned. The cause of consternation was someone with the name Frieda Pinto, who had posted a smiley after a rather silly post by Nags on the beeutiful [sic] weather in Banagallore [sic]. Slyly, Mrs JNR clicked on the postage-stamp-sized photo of Freida and in an instant landed on the latter's page where the lady declared: 'I'm single; I love cooking, dancing and meeting interesting people.'

Later that night, loud noises resounded in the locality along with an imploring male voice outdone by invectives in a shrill, high-pitched, matriarchal voice. That was the last Nags was heard of. Some people even said he had left Bangalore for good. Rohit had a rather uncomfortable feeling that he had caused the act of disappearance and had a sense of foreboding that a season of trouble was ahead at NPS.

CHAPTER 13

Chaos at National Public School

Sidharth and Monica barged into Mrs Chitra Rao's office during a staff meeting, startling everyone in the room. Senior students always got some leeway but this was just not done. The two were panting and in a state of visible panic. Monica blurted out, 'Ma'am, they are fighting!' Mrs Rao slowly rose. She did not like her students fight. Her demeanour signalled seriousness. 'Let me take a look,' said Mrs Mitra, who taught mathematics and was the most feared teacher, implying that she would try to settle matters before Mrs Rao got involved.

'Ma'am, it's serious. I think he is hurt,' said Sidharth, unsure whether he was doing the right thing by providing information that could jeopardize his friends, but he was also overtaken by a sense of urgency. The choice was between giving away and the safety of his friends.

'Who, where?' Mrs Rao was angry and concerned.

'They . . . There . . . Ma'am . . .' Monica was sobbing as she pointed towards the basement, which housed the audio-visual room. Mrs Rao, Mrs Mitra and Mr Rodrigues, the school accountant, rushed out. They could hear screams from the basement. As they barged in, sudden silence fell. Two groups of students stood across them, petrified.

Mrs Rao broke the silence. 'Who is hurt?' Silence.

'I want to know who is hurt.' Her eyes surveyed the fourteen kids, trying in vain to look normal. She saw the boy with a black eye, lurking behind two girls.

'Vikram,' she said with a severity the children had never heard, 'come here!'

Vikram stepped up meekly. He looked dishevelled and drained of energy.

'Who did that?'

Vikram was quiet.

Mrs Rao walked towards Samvartika and demanded, 'Who hit him?'

Samvartika looked down, silently clutching her backpack for support, despairing.

Mrs Rao's face became sterner and everyone was struck with fear at what she might do next.

'Ma'am, I did that.' It was Ashu. The admission startled the group but also brought instant relief. The alternative would have been a lot more agonizing.

'You and you, come to my room. The rest of you, follow Mr Rodrigues to the assembly point and wait there.'

Mrs Rao turned and walked out of the room with Ashu and Vikram trudging like sacrificial goats behind her.

* * *

The trouble started brewing with a rather innocuous conversation between the two groups shortly after the last class, which ended at about 3 p.m. The students were required to do a project, but instead of getting down to their assignment, they had started a rather spirited conversation on business, government, ethics, corruption and the consequent social degeneration. One student had labelled all businessmen as corrupt, unscrupulous and morally defunct. Someone objected to that generalization and said that his dad was a businessman and in calling every businessman as corrupt, the other boy was a jackass.

'Did you call me a jackass?'

'No, a dim-witted, self-centred, vain jackass!'

'You and your stupid businessmen ancestors are a bunch of that!'

'Don't badmouth my ancestors . . .'

'I will if they taught you to call people names!'

Someone shoved somebody. There was palpable tension. And then, things went viral. Everyone in the room took sides, there was a volley of 'you shut up' and '*you* shut up'. Male hormones kicked in and the two boys clashed.

Right now, heads hung in guilt and minds awash with fear, the two stood clumsily in Mrs Rao's room. Their cohorts, worried about their welfare and imagining consequences ranging from suspension to rustication, stood at the assembly point.

***

The entire class was suspended for a day. All the parents were called in and asked what should be done to their wards. Suddenly, the matter was not just about two boys exceeding their limits at the end of an argument gone wrong. Word spread to their homes, relatives were informed, friends had notifications, and the atmosphere was charged, rife with conversations on moral decay to the failure of parenting to over-disciplining young people. Other than making it to the news headlines, it seemed to all the involved parties that this was the most important event after the Big Bang!

On Monday, with the senior class suspended, the entire school was gloomy. Only the kindergarten kids had no idea of what was going on. Mrs Rao was in her own room for the most part but the teacher's common room was abuzz. Everyone wanted a first-hand account from Mrs Mitra. The helpers and other staff members, even the gardeners, had caught a whiff. Everyone wanted to know how the matter would end. It all got resolved when Vikram's dad, a member of the Indian Police Service, called Mrs Rao. People said he was actually a trained hostage negotiator and an expert in counter-terrorism.

'Debate, Ma'am, a healthy massive debate is what we need,' he suggested.

'I don't understand, Mr Singh.'

'That is the issue, Mrs Rao. Neither do I!'

'So, what should we do?'

'Debate, Ma'am, I am telling you. A healthy, massive debate!'

Suddenly it was all clear to her. She asked for a staff meeting.

* * *

Strange how the school felt like a sad place with just a day of suspension for the senior class. In many ways, the class was the school's jewel in the crown. They had lived and breathed the NPS spirit for more than a decade; they had seen teachers come and go and it was they who were to sow the NPS spirit far and wide one day. They had come as tiny tots, barely out of their parent's cuddle, and soon they were going to enter the world to be professionals and entrepreneurs and policymakers and people who would make it a better place for everyone to live in. Even as the suspension was for just a day, it seemed like infinity because no one knew how the issue would be resolved after the class came back. The teachers, who should have loved the unscheduled respite, were actually restless. They simply wanted their kids back; that was what the young ones meant to them.

That is how when the call to meet up with Mrs Chitra Rao came, they all rushed in, eager to ask that everyone move on. As if on cue, Mrs Rao asked everyone to take their seats and after a short review of the events, asked that forgiveness was in order and suggested that in keeping with the great NPS tradition, the students be given a challenge that would prove that from every adversity, it was possible to create a higher good. Mrs Mitra and Mrs Singh were very intrigued with this rather esoteric idea. Then Mrs Rao took off her progressive lenses and peered into the assembly of teachers, cleared her throat and lifted the suspense. 'I believe we should ask the students to get in depth and fight the issue with their intellect and not brute force. I ask that we have a debate in which let the boys and girls take positions on whether business is good or bad for life and living. It is a serious enough issue after all. Why should an NPS senior have ill-informed thoughts on a subject like this and then give vent to emotions slugging another student? Anger is an expression of an ignorant mind, a mind in its own captivity; for wasn't it said famously by someone that understanding is the beginning of freedom? When our boys and girls will understand issues, they will be truly free and respect other people's sense of freedom.'

Mrs Rao was revered by her colleagues for her ability to articulate and she was a great balance between the ideal and the practical. Listening to her, all the teachers perked up, some nodded their head in agreement. The stage was set. Mrs Rao looked around the room for signs of dissent and not finding any, she threw in the challenge. 'I want one of you to take charge. This should be the most significant event of 2012. We want the entire senior school to come and we want their parents to come and let us organize a debate competition like never before.' Even as most of the teachers were taking time to make up their minds, a slender hand went up. It was Prat Rao.

CHAPTER 14

The Great Debate

The auditorium was full of students, teachers, staff members and parents. A big banner across the stage read: 'Is Business Good for The World?' The participants sat in two groups, those in favour and those against, anxiously waiting for the proceedings to commence. Vikram Singh was leading the group in favour, Ashu was leading the other side. Weeks of intense preparation had gone in and today was the culmination. All the parents were keen to hear what their children had to say. Everyone had dressed up formally for the occasion. Mrs Mitra wore her white and blue Kantha saree from Shantiniketan. Mr Rodrigues wore a suit for the first time in fifteen years of service-above-self at NPS. Prat

Rao was seen shuffling up and down, overseeing the last minute things that needed to fall in place for the great event. She was poised, as usual, even as a few boys and girls of class nine, entrusted with the ground arrangements, ran up and down to her on issues like whether the water should be kept on the table or near the podium and if the banner should be pulled a little to the right. Amidst it all, no one realized that at the far end of the auditorium, three figures sat in total silence, invisible to most human eyes. They were Fly High, Polar, and Edward Deming. At this time, Dr G. entered and expressed satisfaction at the overall arrangements. As soon as he took his seat, Prat Rao made the welcome speech and the debate commenced.

The first to go up on stage was Sidharth Sadrangani. He made a powerful argument around the fact that the world population had crossed 7 billion and was growing. He indicated that this trend would not slow down, leave alone reverse itself, until the 2050s. With the population explosion in countries like India and China, more than half consists of young people who require livelihoods. He quoted from books like Edward Glaeser's *Triumph Of The City* to show how more than half the planet is already living in the cities where there could be no agriculture and how, given the irreversible trend of migration, we need millions of new jobs to be created around the world and how this could not be done by governments who have neither the expertise and resources nor the mandate. Thus it was imperative that business played a crucial role in creating employment and providing people with a sense of self-worth so that there is no social strife and there is hope and optimism, so that people have something to look forward to and can raise families and build homes.

The first to argue against the motion was Monica Sadhu. She took up the forceful issue of corruption. Her contention was that business loves corruption and creates a powerful nexus between government and crime to rob civil society of its right to life, liberty and the pursuit of happiness. She exemplified her theory by quoting eloquently from sources like Transparency International and showed how the size of black money had become so large that even the government did not know how to rein it in. She argued that, right from the time of the East India Company, there have been powerful interwoven business cartels that pushed everything from opium to guns to precious metals. Look at the diamond trade, she argued, and see what it has done to poor African people. 'Every diamond we wear is tainted with the blood of the innocent people made to work in difficult, torrid conditions and watched over by armed guards and Alsatian dogs!'

Anvitha went on next. She brought up the issue of food, shelter, medicine and basic amenities like drinking water for the planet's teeming millions. She said she too was swayed for a moment by the passion in Monica but argued that Monica was 'burning the house to roast the pig'. Business, she argued, was a microcosm of the society and reflects at any point in time the collective mental state of a population. She continued that to save the human population, we would need to undo thousands of years of uninformed agricultural practices that damage the environment. Alternative food and drugs must be invented, produced and distributed and all that needs innovation and smart management and business does that best because of the spirit of individualism and free enterprise.

Kamya took the podium and cited disturbing stories of how big business has contributed to environmental disasters. She cited oil spills that have ecologically damaged the environment for decades and strongly criticized the 'corporate masquerade' about caring for the planet and doing good by doing right. She said if business ever learnt anything, the 2011 oil spill near Florida would not have taken place. She then brought home the clout business enjoyed in every country and its capacity to manage legal systems. How else do you explain, she thundered, the men and women behind the Bhopal gas tragedy still being scot-free? Then she talked about use of chemicals and pesticides that are leaving children maimed and unalterably impacting every other species on the planet. She pointed towards the wanton use of plastics and called the landfills of the world the dancing field of the business-Satan.

Rohit brought an interesting new angle to the debate. He cited systems theory to indicate that global problems are no longer simple to decode; they require the engagement of several experts across specializations. Issues like infrastructure, public health and law and order, traditionally in the domain of the government, now require public–private partnerships (PPPs). Increasingly, we are recognizing the impact of such a model. 'Look at India's golden quadrilateral project today. Thanks to the private sector's resources, execution ability and efficiency, India has been able to link up remote corners and only when we are connected and communicating can we thrive as a nation. Without the PPP model, where would the road and telecom infrastructure be?'

To reinforce Kamya's comment on business as Satan, Nivrith blasted the world of business, starting with the role businessmen had played in recent telecom scandals that rocked the country. He argued that business was only in love with itself and always justified the means for the end. He strongly felt that wherever we see evidences of inequality, opportunism, human exploitation and profiteering, business is culpable.

Sowmya Khandelwal was next. She chided her opponent for getting carried away with rhetoric and pointed out the need for giving business its due. She said that communism had not only frowned on business, it had declared free-enterprise the bane of humanity and look where that rhetoric took Russia and East European countries. She then cited the ability of business to make large-scale impact beyond making profits and remarked, without corporate philanthropy many things would not have been possible. She cited the Tatas as an example. Did people know that all the profits various Tata companies make go into the holding entity Tata Sons, which is a trust that invests much of it in social causes? That is how the house of Tatas has given birth to the Indian Institute of Science, Tata Institute of Social Sciences, Tata Memorial Hospital and countless other institutions. She talked about the power of philanthropy, citing the examples of the Rockefeller family, she talked of Warren Buffett and Bill Gates and finally, Azim Premji who donated billions of dollars of personal wealth to help the cause of school education in India. True, there have been transgressions by business houses from time to time, but it is a reflection of a larger social system. Businesses cannot be corrupt in societies that are honest. The bodypolitik is the dog and business its tail. The solution is not in disgracing business but in large social-politico-economic reform.

Pallavi, in a tongue-in-cheek manner, commended business for doing good but chided it for selling things people did not need and for creating a mindset that consumption equals happiness. The more people purchase, the more successful business becomes. As a result, it thrives on a culture of consumption that not only depletes earth's resources but also the capacity to build inner peace in every human being. You have a bike, you need a car. You have a car, you want a better car. You have a better car, you need a second car. It is a rat race and business wants you to be in it so that it can chase its own tail. What the world needs is a bigger set of good people to become doctors and teachers and engineers and not hordes of MBA degree seekers whose job is to make us all worship the false god of consumption.

Finally, Sadhana Sanjay made a passionate case for the idea of entrepreneurship and explained how the spirit of entrepreneurs is very different. They see opportunities where others see problems. To solve the complex problems in the world around us, what we need is pervasive entrepreneurship and, given the kind of interconnectedness we have in today's world, if business did not behave itself and crossed lines, there are enough watchdogs both in the civil society and the government. She also cited examples of self-regulation and urged everyone to build dialogue and not just debate; she argued for engagement and not just demand for compliant behaviour, so that we can all live together in a world of hope and sustainability.

The debate raged like a monsoon downpour that swept the audience in one direction and then the other. Words rained, arguments struck like lightning. Finally, it was time to draw the curtain. Mrs Rao went up to congratulate the two valiant teams who had argued the issue with passion and wisdom and declared the winners amidst thunderous applause. All participants were given a copy of *MBA at 16* by Dr G. and everyone went home happy.

No one noticed the threesome at the far end of the auditorium. They looked at each other in silent approval.

'Let's go,' said Deming's ghost, with an air of great satisfaction. Polar and Fly High got up somewhat reluctantly. This was so much fun but, like everything good, had come to an end. They gently moved out and melted into the night sky.

CHAPTER 15

The Last Word

From my earliest memory of a career conversation in the Bagchi household when Somalingam became a part of me, it has been a long and fascinating journey. I grew up to eventually study political science and then wanted to be a researcher. Instead, by a quirk of fate, I found my first job inside a government office as a clerk. Until that point, I had no idea about the world of business but, shortly after, I joined the DCM group of companies as a management trainee, working in a textile manufacturing plant for the first five years, something I have written about in greater detail in my book, *Go Kiss the World*. With that began a journey of over three decades during which I joined the information technology industry, worked in India and the US, travelled all over the world and returned to co-found MindTree where I currently work. Ours is an industry dominated by the youth. We recruit and train people fresh out of engineering colleges and it appals me how little our young people know or care about the world of business that touches them every day. How I wish they were better informed because in their hands is the future of mankind. But then I also think that we in the world of business have done scant to create interest in our youth, beyond swooping down on talent in droves during recruitment time and then forgetting the world of education for the rest of the year. I also wonder why we should engage young people in a discussion on business only when they are in college? Why not when they are young adults, ready to leave school, when the impressions that get etched in their minds guide them throughout their adult lives? That is the genesis of this book. Rather than give out bookish knowledge or create an exalted piece of academic work, I thought I would write something palatable and something that would kindle their interest, to speak to each other and be better informed while seeking facts, discarding popular notions and building their own worldviews. This book is meant to create informed interest in young men and women well before they are job-ready so that they open their minds to one of the most powerful forces at work in shaping our collective destiny. Every force can have positive and negative influences—it depends on the hand that wields it. My purpose would be served if this book helps to open young minds to the enormous possibility the world of business has to build value for humankind.

If this book makes my readers think afresh, become more curious and open and imaginative, I would consider myself to be privileged.

And now for the all-important question: Should you do a real MBA at some stage or not? If yes, should you do it after gaining work experience or right after graduation? There are no definitive answers. Many great business owners, from Steve Jobs to Bill Gates, from Narayana Murthy to Azim Premji, are not MBAs. Quite clearly, an MBA degree is not critical to starting or owning a business. On the other hand, doing an MBA is a surer way to get a job in a business organization and then, working your way to the top because you have a theoretical base and could relate to many ideas in real life. That said, today's corporations need a whole host of competencies and professionals from many different streams. MBA is not a must. At one time, Microsoft was the top hirer of fresh law graduates in the US. To be a CFO of a company you needed to be a chartered accountant or a cost accountant, not necessarily an MBA. To be a chief technology officer, you should be a scientist or a technologist and there is a whole host of high-paying jobs that require behavioural experts and not MBA graduates.

I am not saying that you don't need to do an MBA. Given a chance, go do it and do it well from a credible institution and do it to learn about the fascinating world of business and not simply to land yourself a job. Internationally, some of the best business schools prefer students with prior work experience and this often helps them have a better appreciation of theory apart from making sure that they do not abandon their basic specialization by doing an MBA. That is how a chemical engineer working in a plant could do an MBA to understand the overall business ethos and principles and then return to take on production management. In India, fresh graduates from many engineering disciplines often join an MBA course with the sole idea of landing a well-paying job. That is how some people end up as investment bankers after studying chemical engineering!

Even if you cannot wait to get some solid work experience before doing your MBA, I would suggest you use every summer during school to take up paid work. Do an internship. Apart from giving you some of your life's best lessons, these interludes will tell you what you are cut out for and what not. Think about that. Lead the herd. Do not join it. Be an MBA by choice, not by chance. Here is wishing you good luck!

And by the way, before you go away, many thanks for buying this book.

Should you want to leave me your thoughts, please visit www.mindtree.com/subrotobagchi.

Did you find the stories from Subroto Bagchi's life, which he tells in *MBA at 16*, fascinating?

You can read a lot more about his fascinating life stories in the national bestseller:

Go Kiss the World
Life Lessons for the Young Professional

by Subroto Bagchi

'Go, kiss the world' were Subroto Bagchi's blind mother's last words to him. These words became the guiding principle of his life.

Subroto Bagchi grew up amidst what he calls the 'material simplicity' of rural and small-town Orissa, imbibing from his family a sense of contentment, constant wonder, connectedness to a larger whole and learning from unusual sources. From humble beginnings, he went on to achieve extraordinary professional success, eventually co-founding MindTree, one of India's most admired software services companies. Through personal anecdotes and simple words of wisdom, Subroto Bagchi brings to the young professional lessons in working and living, energizing ordinary people to lead extraordinary lives.

Go Kiss the World will be an inspiration to 'young India', and to those who come from small-town India, urging them to recognize and develop their inner strengths, thereby helping them realize their own, unique potential.

After reading *MBA at 16*, many of you might feel inspired to set up your own business one day. It's a great idea.

But what really makes a successful entrepreneur? You can find out more in:

The High-Performance Entrepreneur
Golden Rules for Success in Today's World

by Subroto Bagchi

'Highly readable, crisply written inspirational reading for any new Indian entrepreneur'—*Frontline*

Difficult though setting up a business is, becoming a high-performance entrepreneur is harder still. And yet, of the many thousands who try, there are those who go on to become successful; some even graduate to setting up companies that hold their own against the toughest competition, becoming icons of achievement. In *The High-Performance Entrepreneur*, Subroto Bagchi draws upon his own highly successful experience to offer guidance from the idea stage to the IPO level. This includes how to decide when one is ready to launch an enterprise, selecting a team, defining the values and objectives of the company and writing the business plan to choosing the right investors, managing adversity and building the brand. Additionally, in an especially illuminating chapter, Bagchi recounts the systems and values which have made Indian IT companies on a par with the best in the world.

High-performance entrepreneurs create great wealth, for themselves as well as for others. They provide jobs, crucial for an expanding workforce such as India's, and drive innovation. In India as elsewhere, governments have become much more entrepreneur friendly than ever before and the rewards of being a successful entrepreneur are many. More than just a guide, this is a book that will tap the entrepreneurial energy within you.

At work, as in life, it is not enough to be successful—you need to be a professional. That is one of the learnings at the core of *MBA at 16*.

How exactly does one become a professional? When you're a little older, you must read the international bestseller:

The Professional
Defining the New Standard of Excellence at Work

by Subroto Bagchi

'In the new era, where every person's actions have the potential to have a global impact, we must redefine what it means to be a true professional.'

By common definition, a professional is someone who possesses the skills and knowledge necessary to do a job—whether it's a top degree from a prestigious university or simply years of on-the-job training. For centuries, we have relied on this definition to help us determine who is capable and who is not, often assuming that the person with the most professional characteristics is the best one for the job. But every day we see examples of so-called professionals who do more harm than good. How can we weed out the best from the worst when the accepted standards are no longer enough, and when even the most powerful and respected among us cannot be trusted to behave responsibly or ethically? According to Subroto Bagchi, the first step is to redefine what it means to be a professional. Today, it takes more than just aptitude—it takes a commitment to doing what's right, not only for your business, but for society as a whole. The Professional is a must-read for anyone looking for a little clarity in an increasingly blurry world.